The Child Wore Pearls

Morgan Matthews

DEDICATION

For my children

CHAPTER ONE

June sat quietly atop the steps which led to her family's second-story apartment. Just below her feet awaited a day's worth of work to be done at her father's jewelry store. She had grown quite accustomed to opening up the shop during the summer months. Hearing rumblings on the other side of the closed door behind her, she knew there was only a few fleeting moments left before her father was dressed, ready to disrupt her solitude.

She ran her fingers through her thick, brown hair and carefully adjusted her pale green cardigan. She had purchased the top at a secondhand store down the street, as she did nearly all of her current wardrobe.

Though she was tall like her mother, at age seventeen she still had not quite blossomed into womanhood. Her work attire typically consisted of a skirt rising just above the knee, paired with a buttoned-up cardigan in a wide range of colors. No matter the occasion, she always wore her white, high-top Converse sneakers.

June's mother never could understand her only child's fashion choices, particularly when it came to her oversized retro-wingtip glasses. As the years passed, she had seemingly given up the fight, and resorted to mere snarky quips every now and again concerning her daughter's appearance. June had learned to ignore such comments, as she knew retaliation would never be a viable option.

"Lorraine! Have you seen my watch?" she heard her father ask, heavy footsteps pacing the kitchen floor behind her. The relationship she shared with the patriarch of their family was considerably warmer than the challenging dynamic she had with her mother. He was both down-to-earth and charming – a salesman through and through. It was from him that June had acquired most of her business savvy. She wondered how he could possibly misplace his watch, it being the only piece of jewelry he donned personally.

His attire consisted of a long-sleeved denim shirt, paired with blue jeans of a very similar hue, which he wore every day of the week. He did, however, always check to make sure he chose a button-up with no visible holes or bleach stains for church services every Sunday morning.

She knew that her father fastening his watch was the last of his morning rituals, and that once it was located, the work day would soon begin. Her mother, on the other hand, likely wouldn't be down for another hour or so. Her morning routine took a bit more time and effort than that of June or her father. Lorraine had worked at a local mall selling and applying makeup as a teenager. She had continued to hone her skills over the years, never leaving the apartment without full glam, as well as hair which had been curled, teased, and hair sprayed – a style which she'd adopted in the mid-90's.

Lorraine's mornings consisted of meticulously placing clothing items on her bed – matching outfits with coordinating jewelry. The pristine collection of necklaces, bracelets, and rings her mother had amassed over the years was undeniably extensive. There was not a birthday, Mother's Day, or anniversary that went by she didn't claim a piece of jewelry in the shop as her own. Even a random Tuesday could be cause for adding to her assortment.

June began her descent to the shop - counting each step, as she did every morning. She took a moment to enjoy the cooler temperature as she reached the bottom. She had always appreciated their store in this time of loneliness, before customers crowded in for the day. The glass counters were nearly barren, as they were every morning. The sun shone through the windows, revealing every speck of dust she may have missed from the day before. As she headed to a nearby cabinet to fetch the glass cleaner, she could hear her father's footsteps as he made his way downstairs.

She began each day by wiping down the glass jewelry counters, vacuuming the floors, and making sure all the shop's lights were switched on – a task which she saved until after the cleaning was done, as it somehow seemed more peaceful with only the light streaming in from the windows to guide her efforts. Next, she would make her way over to the large, green safe located next to her father's office. As she passed, she spotted him sitting at his desk, likely catching up on paperwork. A small, unassuming sign hung on the door which read, "Edward Randolph, Jeweler."

Opening the safe, she gazed upon the dozens of rows of black, velvet trays which contained virtually their shop's entire inventory of merchandise – organized via category of jewelry. She knew exactly where each tray was to be placed so that customers could easily find what they were looking for as they stared through the glass countertops.

A man of large stature, Edward towered over his daughter as he joined in the task of stocking counters for the day.

"Mornin' June Bug. How'd ya sleep?" he asked, placing his hand on her shoulder.

"I slept fine. Wish the Camdens could keep their TV down though."

"Well, their kids don't know what it's like to get up early in the summer," he said. "Bet they get paid for cleaning their own rooms."

June gave her father a knowing look as they continued setting up for the day. As the clock inched closer to opening time, she decided to check that the mini-fridge was fully stocked. She quickly counted the bottles of water, knowing how many her father liked to have on hand to offer patrons as they made their way out of the summer sun. It was then that she climbed the steps back up to their second-story apartment to grab another case.

As she opened the door at the top of the stairs, she could hear music blasting from her mother's bedroom. Tanya Tucker singing "Delta Dawn" filled every corner of their home as June made her way to the kitchen pantry. As she rummaged past the half-eaten bags of chips and canned goods, she noticed the music had been turned down to the point of being barely audible. In its place came the voice of her mother, clearly not speaking to June.

"I don't understand why this is taking so long…" she heard as her mother's voice had now completely drowned out all traces of Tanya Tucker.

"I don't want to hear that you've hit a dead end…"

It was abundantly clear that Lorraine did not know her daughter had returned to the apartment. For a moment, she considered what to do. Should she try and sneak back downstairs? Purposefully drop a can of tomato soup so that her mother would be made aware of her presence… and then of course pretend she'd heard nothing when confronted? Instead, she stood in stunned silence at the kitchen pantry, holding bottles of water in both hands, as well as squeezed under her arms.

"Tell me what I'm paying you for!" Lorraine exclaimed, before the sound of something being hurled into the bedroom wall echoed throughout their home.

June wasn't entirely sure she could move her body even if she tried. She wanted nothing more than to get out of there, but her brain didn't seem to be communicating that message to her legs. Unable to process her mother's not-so-private conversation, the lyrics of Lorraine's favorite song filled the apartment louder than before, as Tanya Tucker was once again the only voice to be heard. She seized the opportunity to quietly make her way back downstairs, once again welcomed by the silence of her father's shop just before it opened for the day.

As she finished up the last of her morning tasks, she could hear her mother's words still ringing in her ears. *Who could she have been talking to? What has hit a dead end?* These were all questions she knew she couldn't possibly answer based solely on the conversation she was not meant to be privy to. She had very little, if any, context to work with when it came to trying to figure out anything having to do with Lorraine Randolph. Her mother was not a terrible person, nor would June describe her as being a negligent parent. She and Lorraine simply were not close.

She could recall that her mother was much more attentive to her as a young child, which, as she thought about it, made perfect sense. *Younger kids need their parents more than teenagers, don't they?* Besides, now being fully capable of caring for herself, June understood that different personality types exist in the world – and not all of those personalities are going to complement one another, even as a mother-daughter relationship. Lorraine had always made sure that June had everything she needed. She may not have been a fan of her simple clothes or lack of hairstyle, but she did seem to care about her daughter, in her own way.

Edward Randolph could always be counted upon as a mediator between his wife and daughter, seemingly communicating with each of them with a great amount of ease and understanding. Where Lorraine and June struggled to connect, Edward filled in the gaps. His topics of conversation were never in short supply, always finding a way to connect their vastly different ways of seeing the world. They say that 'familiarity breeds contempt,' and June felt certain this was at least partially to blame when it came to herself and her mother.

As she found herself lost in thought, wiping down counters she'd already cleaned, and straightening trays of jewelry which were perfect to begin with, she heard her father's voice, though she couldn't make out the words.

"I'm sorry, what did you say?"

"I said it's time to unlock the doors, June Bug."

As she walked to the front of the shop, she heard the sound of music playing once again. Stepping outside, she could see that the hot dog vendor was setting up for the day. While he was only there during the summertime, he always made his presence known on their typically quiet street. This being his first day back since the end of the previous summer, she was happy to see him. He always brought a nice change of pace to the neighborhood, and as Edward put it, "Them hot dogs come with all the fixins' you can think of."

As June wondered who could possibly eat a hot dog so early in the morning, she remembered – *the lemonade!* While there may not have been many hot dogs sold until lunchtime, just as soon as the shops were open and customers had decided to venture out, that man could sell lemonade "like it had healing powers," as her father would say. The summers were hot, and a $3.25 cup of lemonade was perfect for cooling you down while wandering in and out of the mostly 'mom and pop' establishments along the streets. While antique stores were a staple in their town, so were homemade goods such as children's clothing, scented candles, and handcrafted wood furniture.

Fortunately for the Randolph family, they were the only jewelry store for miles, though not if you counted jewelry made from painted sea shells and multi-colored beads - *but why would you?* If you were in the market for diamonds and gold, Randolphs was the place to go. Not only did Mr. Randolph sell jewelry, he also made it. Should a young man want a custom engagement ring made from scratch, that is where Edward could really showcase his talent.

June's talent, on the other hand, was helping people figure out what they wanted. The customers trusted her, and valued her opinion. Whether they be shopping for a gift, or browsing for the perfect piece to justify a splurge for themselves, June could always be counted on for guidance.

"Dad, Mr. Haygood is back. Would you want a lemonade?"

"Oh really? I think I'll stick with my coffee for now, but you go ahead," he said, picking up a large, chipped coffee mug. June had made the mug for him in a pottery class as a child. It donned about twelve different patterns and colors, none of which coordinated.

Crossing the street, she could see that several other shop owners were opening their doors for the day, propping them open with door stoppers and placing chalkboard signs in front which read, "Summer Sale – 20% Off," and, "Roasted Pecans – $3.99/bag or 2 for $6.99." She could see that the clothing boutique next to the wood furniture store had yet to open, as the owner was a bit more flexible with her hours than most. While Mathilde's Boutique and Salon was undeniably busting at the seams with stunning clothes, shoes, and accessories for women, it was entirely too expensive for June's taste.

Of course, her mother was a frequent customer at both the boutique and the connecting hair salon. While expense did, indeed, play a factor in her avoidance of Mathilde's, she wasn't in the habit of spending much of her summer pay — so she likely could afford *something* from the shop should she desire.

June had never quite seen herself as a girl that should wear anything which might draw unnecessary attention. When she did happen upon something which ventured from her typical style, but yet she found herself attracted to — the phrase, "*I couldn't pull it off,*" would inevitably come to mind.

As she approached the hot dog stand, Mr. Haygood greeted her with a smile as he quipped, "Still workin' for the man, I see." She couldn't help but laugh as he poured her a glass of lemonade.

"Well, next year I'll be a senior, so this may be my last summer at home," she responded.

"Maybe so… but you'll be back. That jewelry shop blood is just coursing through your veins, dear."

"I guess we'll see," she replied, grinning.

"Your dad has got himself one of the finest establishments in this town. Not a bad setup if you ask me."

"I don't mind it," she replied. "Of course, it's all I know. I'm hoping college will help me figure that out… what I'd really like to do."

"Yep. Well, I know you've got a knack for retail. It's good to see you again, June."

As she finished up her lemonade, Mr. Haygood insisted she take a refill "for the road." Although she had intended to take her time and enjoy the brief outing, in an effort to get her mind off her mother's conversation earlier in the morning, she could see from a distance they were getting their first customers of the day. She headed back across the street, hoping to feel more at ease once she was caught up in the hustle and bustle of the work day. There was not a lot of time to sit with one's thoughts when there were customers to be helped, as she well knew.

Entering the shop, she could see that her father was helping a young couple browsing engagement rings. "This here is a radiant-cut diamond," he said as he handed the bride-to-be a ring sporting a white gold band and large center stone. Placing her lemonade beneath the counter, she made her way over to the couple.

"June Bug! This young lady here says she's a fan of white gold, but she's not sure yet what shape she's looking for in a center stone – how 'bout you show her some options."

"No problem!" she exclaimed, as her father made his way over to help another customer. After introducing herself to the couple, she learned that they were already in the process of planning a wedding for the fall, but wanted to pick out an engagement ring and wedding bands together. The bride worked as a photographer and loved the idea of an outdoor wedding with fall colors as the backdrop. The groom smiled along as his fiancé described in detail her plans for their big day.

"We have several engagement rings in our case of antique jewelry if you'd like to take a look." At this, the bride's eyes lit up with excitement, confirming for June that she was on the right track. As they made their way to the other side of the shop, she could see that the gentleman her father had been helping was looking in their direction as he browsed the glass counters. Looking up at him, she smiled politely as she and the young couple reached the vintage pieces.

As she had anticipated, the bride-to-be quickly locked eyes on an engagement ring which dated back to the 1920's. She barely had it on her finger before proclaiming its perfection, while beaming from ear to ear. As they discussed the specifics of the ring, June noticed once again that the only other customer in the shop was looking their way. Assuming he was simply amused by the young woman's enthusiasm, she once again smiled politely.

June could see that the man, whom she presumed to be in his late fifties, was nicely dressed, sporting a buttoned-up shirt and tie, despite the summer heat. His hair was wavy and thick, though she saw no hint as to what the original color might have been, as it was completely white. He wore a Rolex watch on his wrist, as well as a simple wedding band on his left hand. She wondered if he was shopping for a gift for his wife, as she could see he was currently admiring the pearl necklaces, which were housed in a counter near the front of the shop.

After speaking in private for a few moments, the couple decided on the engagement ring, but said they would return another day to shop for wedding bands. June reiterated her excitement for them, and complimented the bride on her selection. Seeing that her father had emerged from his office, she called him over to assist them in sizing their new purchase.

Focusing her attention on the older gentleman still browsing, she grabbed a drink from the mini-fridge and made her way over to offer it to him.

"Looks like summer starts early around here. It's not even June yet and I find myself looking around for a snow cone truck," he said as he took a swig of water.

June laughed as she reached for the cup of lemonade still waiting for her under the counter.

"Yes, sir. Did you just move here?"

"I did. It's a fine town. I'll just need a little time to adjust to this heat, I suppose."

"Yeah, it's not so bad once you've been here a while," she said, taking a sip of her drink.

"Have you lived here long?"

"All my life," she answered with a grin.

"That must be nice, though, living in a place so familiar. My wife and I have moved a lot throughout the years, truth be told."

"Well, we're glad to have you guys. My dad owns the shop… so if you have any questions, just let me know," she said with a grin, as she heard the sound of the apartment door opening at the top of the stairs.

It was then that she noticed her customer's face was turning a bit pale, and that his eyes were fixated on something located just behind her. She turned to see that her mother had emerged from the bottom of the stairs. June turned once again to look at the man on the other side of the counter, yet he continued to stand in stunned silence. After a few moments, he mumbled something about needing to get home, apologized, and headed quickly out the front door – disappearing into the glare of the summer sun.

CHAPTER TWO

Later that evening, June listened intently as the sound of rainfall could be heard just outside her bedroom window. *Maybe if I tell them I'm sick I won't have to get up for dinner*, she thought as she maneuvered the sneakers off her tired feet. Suddenly feeling the full weight of the day, she turned onto her side and repositioned the pillow under her head.

As she looked around the room, she could see that her bookshelf, which housed hundreds of novels of varying genres, was in desperate need of organizing. Although she generally rejected the idea of holding onto a lot of material possessions, she found it difficult to let go of the stories and characters which had kept her company throughout her childhood years. While her bookshelf did, indeed, contain books which she had read more recently, a lot of room was devoted to those which were no longer age-appropriate.

She had developed a habit early on in childhood of finishing every day enthralled in a story, which she happily used as a means of escaping her mundane existence. She couldn't possibly recall the many nights spent straining her eyes, in an effort to stay awake to finish a chapter. It seemed as if her mother was always trying to catch her up past bedtime. "Lights out, June!" were the words she dreaded most as a child desperate for an outlet to the outside world.

Now at age seventeen, she no longer felt the need to quickly stuff her book under her pillow and switch off the tableside lamp when she heard footsteps making their way down the hall towards her room. Having to get up for either school or work the next morning was motivation enough to know when it was time to call it quits.

She wondered if diving into a new biography, which she'd recently acquired at the secondhand store, would be enough of a distraction to quiet her currently-racing thoughts. Considering the events of the day, June felt undeniably drained. She had never felt as though she and her mother would get to the point of sharing personal details of their lives with one another on a regular basis. She did, however, feel as though she knew Lorraine about as well as anyone ever could, besides perhaps her father.

Lorraine was not one to pursue close relationships with others. Nevertheless, she did have a group of ladies whom she met with one evening a week to play 'Bunco' and engage in frivolous gossip. Occasionally, she would spill the proverbial 'beans' to Edward when the topic of conversation had been particularly juicy, which June often overheard.

Should the Machen's eldest son have been caught by police vandalizing street signs, Lorraine Randolph was the first to know. Though June had to admit she couldn't know for sure whether or not her mother's relationships with one or more of these women had extended past the surface level, she had a hunch that Lorraine was content with 'Bunco talk,' and pursued nothing more.

When it came to her mother's family history, she didn't know much. This seemed as if Lorraine's preference. She never met her maternal grandmother, as she passed a few years prior to June's birth. While her grandfather did pay them a visit for a few days every year or two, he lived on the opposite side of the country. Travel had grown increasingly difficult for him with age.

As June was reminded many times throughout the years, Lorraine's parents had been told they would never be able to have children. They went on to eventually conceived in their mid-forties. As Lorraine described it, she was her mother's 'miracle baby,' and the apple of her father's eye.

While her grandfather could not be physically present in her life growing up, he always found ways to let his only granddaughter know that he cared for her. Though he was not a wealthy man, he always sent a check for June's college savings every birthday and Christmas. When she had posed the idea of traveling to visit him, her mother would typically reply that they couldn't close the shop for an extended period of time, as they employed no one who could take over in their absence. June had always felt that her father would have been fine with closing shop for a few days in order to visit, but he simply nodded in agreement as his wife brushed off any suggestion of a trip.

As she contemplated her mother's lack of social connections, she considered the possibility of reaching out to her. *Could she be in some kind of trouble?* Though their relationship was far from cozy, June cared deeply for the woman who had raised her. Despite her many flaws, she had always felt that her mother was doing the best she knew how.

Lorraine was only eighteen when her mother passed away – *could that be the source of her disconnect?* She wondered if there was any way she might begin to chip away at the wall her mother had built between them. *Maybe I never tried hard enough,* she thought as she buried her face into her hands. At this, she became aware of the sound of footsteps, dreading the forthcoming knock at her door.

"Dinner's on the table. I ordered you that shrimp toast you like," Edward said as he peaked his head around the door.

"Thanks. I'll be there in a minute."

"You under the weather, June Bug?"

For a moment, she considered seizing the opportunity to stay in bed and avoid her mother altogether.

"No, I'm fine. I'll be right there."

As she made her way towards the kitchen, she could smell the aroma of spaghetti and meatballs. Delivery from Anthony's Restaurant was, at a minimum, a weekly occurrence in the Randolph household. As Lorraine wasn't a big fan of cooking, their weekly dinner menus were located in a kitchen drawer next to the stove – all the local restaurants that delivered were in the rotation.

As she took a seat next to her father, she could see that Lorraine was standing in the living room, feather duster in hand. Her mother was just finishing up her evening routine of carefully dusting the collection of Fenton art glass which she housed in a glass curio cabinet.

The cabinet came complete with lighting which further showcased her prized art. Every piece in Lorraine's collection was an antique, as June was reminded many times as a young child. She had always found herself mesmerized by her mother's collection of glass bowls, figurines, dishes, bottles, and vases.

The colors were stunning, and the designs intricate and beautiful. They were always on display, but never to be touched by anyone other than Lorraine. As she got older, and thus capable of understanding the importance of exercising extreme caution when handling the glass, June had offered multiple times to assist her mother with the care of her collection, but to no avail. *She doesn't trust me with anything – she never will.*

"The cabinet looks beautiful, Mom. I was admiring your new piece earlier today."

Lorraine looked at her daughter as if she had thrown a meatball in her direction rather than a simple compliment as to the state of her curio cabinet.

"You've never taken an interest in the glass," her mother replied as she fixed herself a plate of spaghetti.

"I've just never taken the time to really appreciate it, I guess."

"Well, remember not to touch the cabinet, June. If you want to help with something there's a pile of clean laundry just waiting to be put away."

At this, Edward chimed in. "I remember when we bought your first piece, Lorraine. It was that one shaped kind of like a perfume bottle, you remember?"

Lorraine nodded as she opened a gallon of sweet tea and poured herself a glass. Looking down at her plate of shrimp toast and spaghetti, June couldn't help but feel discouraged at the prospect of ever seeing a thaw in her mother's icy exterior. *Could Dad know what she's up to?* The thought had barely crossed her mind before it was answered by Edward himself.

"Oh hey, I meant to ask you earlier, Lorraine – do you know what happened to the bedroom wall? Saw a hole in the drywall, next to the TV."

Lorraine's eyes darted abruptly to her husband, who was clearly unaware of the tension he had inadvertently brought to the dinner table. June sat silently, hanging on her mother's every movement as Lorraine awkwardly brought her glass of tea to her lips. *Is this a stalling tactic?* As she eagerly awaited her mother's response, June found herself desperately hoping that the exchange would offer any amount of insight into her mother's conversation earlier in the day. *What did she throw at the wall? Her phone? What could have made her so angry?*

Lorraine slowly lowered her glass of tea back onto the table.

"Oh yeah, I tripped earlier today as I was getting dressed. My elbow hit the wall when I tried to catch myself," she replied.

"Are you okay?" Edward inquired. As June studied her father's face, she saw not even the slightest hint of doubt as to her mother's explanation, only the look of genuine concern.

"Yes, fine."

As she sat, listening intently, June recalled a time when her mother had tripped after walking on uneven sidewalk. The fall had left her with a nasty bruise on her leg, and resulted in a fair amount of pampering by her doting husband. She had not been the least bit shy in reminding her family of the bruise on a daily basis, and subsequently soliciting opinions as to whether or not the size and color were improving.

She found it peculiar that as her mother described the incident, which supposedly resulted in damage to the bedroom wall, she failed to produce any evidence of an injury. As she secretly hoped that her father would ask to see Lorraine's elbow, her mother quickly changed the subject.

"How'd the shop make out today?"

As Edward answered his wife, June focused her attention onto her shrimp toast, which was undoubtedly getting cold. She found herself increasingly confused and frustrated by her mother's deception, which served as a reminder as to why she was generally uncomfortable with concerning herself in other's affairs. Being described at times as a 'people pleaser,' she had grown accustomed to staying out of her mother's way, as June was confident that was Lorraine's preference as well.

"Thank you for dinner. I think I'll get to bed now," she said as she made her way over to the sink.

"Tired, Bug?" her father asked.

"Yes, sir."

Upon clearing her plate, she headed back down the hallway, relieved to be free of her parents' company.

As she was welcomed by the comfort of her quiet room, June plopped down onto her bed – a bed in which she'd slept since the age of four. Reaching for her cell phone which sat on the bedside table, she couldn't help but long for some sort of distraction.

As she scrolled through her Facebook feed, she could see that most of her friends were already enjoying their summer vacations, most of them at the beach. Her family, on the other hand, rarely traveled.

Her father enjoyed visiting a town about two hours away, which hosted a yearly watermelon festival. It was difficult, however, to convince her mother to take even a short, weekend getaway.

As she wondered if they would make the trip to the festival later in the summer, she couldn't help but smile as memories of the town's local bed-and-breakfast came to mind. They always stayed at the same one – *the one with the giant porch swing out front.* It was on that swing where she would cover both herself and her parents with a blanket in the evenings. The three of them would sit together and talk, all while enjoying the watermelon they'd purchased earlier in the day. Even Lorraine, it seemed, was not immune to the calming effect of that porch swing.

June reached under her bed in search of a shoe box which contained photographs she'd saved throughout the years. Her mother did not particularly like to take pictures, nor did she keep photo albums. Edward was old-school when it came to photography, preferring to use disposable cameras purchased at the drug store to capture his family. As she rummaged through the box, she stopped to admire photos of herself as an infant. In one such image, Lorraine stood in front of their living room fireplace, cradling June in her arms.

Looking at the photos, she couldn't help but see the resemblance between herself and her mother. Despite their physical characteristics, which were undeniably similar, June struggled to feel as though her own looks would ever compare. Lorraine had always been a beautiful woman. She was tall, slender, and her fair, freckled skin somehow offered the perfect contrast to her long, dark hair.

June had always admired her mother's hair, which was several shades darker than her own. As a child, she would watch as she fashioned her locks into the perfect 'messy' bun atop her head before completing household chores. She couldn't understand why her mother never wore her hair like that in public. While Lorraine could certainly draw attention with her carefully applied makeup and teased hairstyle, June had always preferred the way she looked at home.

It was then that she happened upon a photo of herself as a toddler. She wore a Cinderella costume complete with kid-sized, sparkly heels and a shiny tiara. As she gazed upon the old photograph, trying in vain to recall the day, she heard a knock at her bedroom door. She returned the photos to the shoebox as quickly as possible before searching frantically for the lid. She located the top hiding under a nearby pillow before stuffing the box back under her bed.

"Come in."

"Just wanted to check on you – thought you were quiet at dinner," her father said as he made his way into the room.

"I'm sorry. I'm sure I'll feel better by morning. It's just been a long day."

To her surprise, he took a seat at the foot of the bed. As if to make time before deciding what to say next, he cleared his throat and awkwardly adjusted his wristwatch. Edward Randolph was not a man that was typically comfortable with discussing the complexities of human emotion. While he may have been the first to ask how you're doing, anything other than a surface level answer would have caused him to quickly retreat out of sheer embarrassment. He was, however, very aware that his wife was similarly lacking in this area. He had always done his best to ensure that his daughter had someone to talk to, should she have the need.

"I just… want to make sure you're doing okay, June Bug. Hope I'm not workin' ya too hard."

"No, Dad – really, I'm doing fine. I'd let you know if there was a problem."

"Alright, well you just tell me if you need some time off this summer. I can hold down the fort just fine on my own. I know you may have some things you'd like to do."

"I appreciate that. Thanks, Dad."

Edward smiled, seemingly reassured by his daughter's response.

"Oh, by the way, did that man in the tie ever say what he was looking for today?" he asked. "Told me he was just browsing, but he was looking for a while."

June recalled the odd encounter she'd had with the older gentleman earlier in the day. Having expended most of her mental energy on the situation with her mother, she hadn't really thought much about the man in the tie. After all, working in customer service for as long as she had, she was relatively used to behavior which some might deem 'outside the norm.'

She did, however, find it curious that his decision to leave so suddenly seemed to coincide with her mother's appearance in the store. Though, as she knew it could have been any number of reasons, she decided it wasn't worth mentioning to her father.

"No, he never said he was looking for anything in particular. He just moved here, so he's probably checking out all the shops in town."

"I got ya. Well, goodnight darlin.' See you in the morning," he said, giving her a reassuring smile as he made his way to the door.

Upon his departure, June lay motionless on her bed, her right hand resting gently at her chest. She and her father had applied dozens of glow-in-the-dark stars to her bedroom ceiling several years prior, which still remained. Though as a teenager she found them to be a bit tacky, she felt strangely comforted as she looked up at them. Her eyes grew heavy as she fell into a deep sleep, listening to the sound of the ceiling fan turning above her bed.

CHAPTER THREE

The next morning, June tried in vain to be attentive as her father brainstormed ways in which they might update the front window display of the shop. Though typically invested in every aspect of the business, she couldn't help but feel disconnected as she quietly wiped down the glass jewelry counters.

"What says 'summer' to you?" he asked, tinkering with their existing display.

"I don't know, Dad. The sun?" June retorted with a grin.

"I know you're being cute, but that's a good idea! Think you could make a big sun to go up in the corner?"

"Make a sun out of what?" she asked, hoping he was just making a joke in response to her sarcasm.

"I was kind of hoping you might have an idea."

Realizing her father wouldn't be content until he felt the shop was 'summer-ready,' she conceded to the fact that she would be taking the lead on revamping the window display. "Let me look up some ideas later and I'll get back to you on it."

"Thanks, June."

As opening time rolled around, she headed to the front of the shop. Looking out the window, she could see that there were considerably more shoppers flooding the sidewalks than the day before. One such shopper caught her eye – a man chatting with Mr. Haygood at the hot dog stand as he sipped his lemonade. The man was tall, nicely dressed, and sported a head full of thick, white hair. The sleeves of his buttoned-up dress shirt had been rolled to just below his elbows, with his Rolex watch clearly visible, even at a distance.

She quickly realized the man standing with Mr. Haygood was the same man she had met in the shop the day before. She never could understand why he had left so suddenly, but hoped they hadn't somehow made a bad impression on a potential new customer.

The day was shaping up to be just like any other. Customers trickled in, slowly at first – most just 'counter' shopping, as her father put it, with no intention to buy. Though as she started to put away a display of necklaces, she heard a familiar voice coming from the front of the shop.

"Looks like they're open."

It was Ethan Morris, a boy from June's class. He was standing in front of the shop door as several of his friends made their way inside. She hated when Ethan came into the shop. Though an undeniably handsome guy, June couldn't help but feel that he was sorely lacking in humility. He and his friends spent their summers running the roads in their jacked-up trucks, paid for by their wealthy parents.

Though she had a small circle of friends, June mostly kept to herself. She certainly had never been invited to hang out with the girls that Ethan and his friends typically ran around with. As the guys had a lot of time on their hands, she was used to them occasionally stopping by the shop and subtly giving her a hard time.

Ethan smiled as he made his way over to the counter.

"I'm in the market for a new watch. Think your dad would buy my old one from me?" Ethan asked as he motioned to the watch on his wrist.

"I'm not sure. I'd have to ask him," she replied, peeking around the corner at her father's office. She could see him sitting at his desk, talking on the phone while scribbling on his notepad.

"He'll be just a few minutes. Can I show you some watches while you're waiting?" she asked, praying her father would soon be off his phone call and able to take over.

"No, I think I'll wait on your old man for that. You could show me some rings, though."

"Rings?"

"Yeah. Told my dad I'd text him some pictures if I saw any rings my mom might like for their anniversary," Ethan said as he adjusted his baseball cap.

June noticed some of Ethan's friends snickering in the background, whispering to one another behind cupped hands. Though she was generally unfazed by their immaturity, she found herself feeling suddenly self-conscious. *What could they be laughing about?*

"Sure, no problem," she said, making her way over to a nearby jewelry counter. "Just let me know what I can take out for you."

At this, Ethan's friends burst into laughter, no longer attempting to mask their buffoonery. June could feel as her cheeks grew hotter by the second and pressure began to build behind her eyes. Keeping a straight face, she waited patiently while Ethan browsed the counter. She tried desperately to continue breathing at a steady pace. Her anxiety was mounting with every passing second. Glancing toward her father's office, she wanted nothing more than an opportunity to flee.

"Let me see that one," Ethan said, pointing at a ring which featured a large, solitaire diamond and white gold band.

"This one?"

Ethan nodded as she pulled the ring from beneath the counter.

"You know, this is an engagement ring. We have several anniversary bands in this section… if you think that may be what your dad is looking for," she said politely.

"I *know* what he's looking for," he replied, holding the ring mere inches from his face, as if to study the center stone.

Ethan knows nothing about diamonds. Who does he think he's fooling?

"What do you think of this one, guys?" he asked, turning his back toward June, inviting his friends to admire the piece.

June had resolved to the fact that she needed to treat her classmate just as she would any other customer, despite her frustration concerning his attitude. Though the boys had mistakenly identified the diamond as being princess-cut, she managed to resist the urge to correct them. She didn't want to run the risk of coming across as rude, so she waited patiently as her male classmates talked amongst themselves, each offering various remarks. Though as the minutes passed, June couldn't help but wonder why Ethan had still failed to send a photo of the ring to his father.

"I can take a picture for you if you like. I could put it in a box first – to me that always looks better to have that black backdrop," she offered, hoping to speed up the process a bit.

"No, that's okay, I don't think he'd be interested in this one. None of these are really up to our standards when it comes to jewelry," Ethan replied smugly as he placed the ring back on the counter. "Guess we'll have to drive a bit out of our way to find a quality jewelry store." He turned once again to his friends as they started to make their way toward the front door.

June watched as the boys snickered amongst themselves. Their incessant whispering to one another reminded her of middle school shenanigans. Though exasperated by Ethan's comments, June felt relieved that the interaction was finally at an end. All she wanted was to get back to helping other customers.

As she gazed down at the engagement ring, she felt the blood suddenly drain from her face. Picking it up from the counter, her hands began to shake uncontrollably. She tried to keep breathing, but it was no use.

"STOP!"

June's voice cracked slightly as she spoke. She felt just as angry as she did fearful in that moment. Though she didn't want to believe it, she knew from the moment she laid eyes on the piece of jewelry sitting atop the glass counter that it was not the ring which belonged to the shop. The ring she held in her hand was, in fact, costume jewelry which could be purchased at any department store for around ten dollars. She had seen similar knockoffs the last time she visited the mall, sold near the handbags and women's shoe department. These rings came in various designs, and looked very realistic to the untrained eye.

It suddenly occurred to June *why* Ethan had asked to see that particular ring – it looked the most like the fake he was carrying with him. He had likely chosen as simple a design as possible, increasing his chances of finding a similar piece among the rows of jewelry at Randolphs. While she had been warned of this tactic previously by her father, she had never encountered it personally. *I shouldn't have let him turn his back to me*, she thought, as the seriousness of what was happening started to set in. *I'm about to accuse Ethan Morris of stealing… I'm going to have to call the police! WHAT is he doing!?*

Ethan and his friends stood just inside the doorway of Randolphs, looking as though they were deer which had been caught in the headlights of one of their jacked-up pickup trucks. After what seemed like an eternity, Ethan broke the silence. "What is it,

Randolph? We got to get going." He then turned once again to leave. As June was about to order them to stay put, she heard the voice of a man standing somewhere to her right break in.

"Hold it right there, boys!"

The voice was that of an older gentleman – her customer from the day before. He stood looking squarely at Ethan and his crew from only a few feet away. The sleeves of his buttoned-up shirt were still rolled to just below his elbows, as they were when she had seen him earlier in the day. His expression gave June the feeling that she wouldn't be alone in this situation.

"Let's everyone just head back on in here," he said as he directed them to move forward.

As the boys' motionless bodies began to inch closer to the man giving the orders, Edward suddenly emerged from his office and made his way towards the commotion. He wore a look of concern as he stood next to his daughter.

"What seems to be the problem, June?" Edward asked.

She knew that it was the moment of truth – she would be accusing her classmates of a serious crime which would likely result in one of the biggest scandals their small town had ever seen. Looking down at the ring she still held in her hands, she could feel her stomach begin to turn.

"I was showing these guys one of our engagement rings. This is what they returned to me," she said, handing her father the knockoff. Edward adjusted his eyeglasses, as they had a habit of slipping toward the end of his nose. As he took a closer look at the ring, June glanced over at the nicely dressed customer who had come to her aid. He was not taking his eyes off of Ethan and his friends, seemingly ready to spring into action should they try anything. She wondered how she had failed to notice him enter the shop.

Edward cleared his throat as he placed the ring on the counter. "Well, I don't believe that's one of our rings, boys."

"Sh… sure it is, Mr. Randolph. That's the ring June gave me to look at," Ethan said as he looked nervously at his friends, none of them chiming in.

June remained silent as her father glared at the young man standing before him.

"Okay. I think it's about time we let the police handle this," he said, turning to face his daughter. Though he'd planned on instructing her to make the call, Edward could see the fear and apprehension in the eyes of his only child. It was then that he realized what June had already considered – the impact this would have on her.

"June, why don't you help those customers for me," he said as he nodded toward a middle-aged couple standing near the antique jewelry. The pair were clearly hanging on every word of the scene unfolding in front of them. As she made her way toward the couple, she took one last look at Ethan. The boy standing in her father's shop seemed so far from the cocky, privileged teenager she knew. He was pale, nervous, and seemingly trying to burn a hole through the floor, as he refused to take his eyes off the beige carpet just below his feet.

"Sir, would you mind keeping an eye on these boys as I make that phone call in my office?" Edward asked, speaking to the man who had stepped in to assist June.

"Not at all," he replied.

Edward once again picked up the ring in question before hurriedly making his way to his office. June wondered if Ethan would willingly give up the real ring once the police had arrived, or if she and all of their customers would be witness to a dramatic search of her classmates. As she got back to work helping customers, she couldn't help but feel relieved that, at least for the moment, she was removed from the situation.

The next hour seemed to pass in a bit of a blur. The police arrived at the shop quickly. An officer approached June privately to take her statement, for which she was very grateful. It was somehow a relief to know she wouldn't have to, yet again, accuse Ethan and his friends to their faces. Though keeping her distance, she overheard the nicely dressed customer identify himself to police. He had stuck around after officers arrived to offer his account of the day's events.

It didn't take much questioning before Ethan willingly offered up the diamond ring, which he'd hidden in the pocket of his jeans. The other guys held their heads as one by one their parents were called.

Officers eventually escorted the boys into the backs of their patrol cars, informing Edward that they would be transported to the police station where they would be met by their parents.

June couldn't help but once again consider the impact this incident would likely have on their town. She was fairly certain that Ethan's mother regularly attended the same weekly Bunco game that Lorraine frequented. Though she knew there was nothing she could have done differently in the situation, she worried that she could somehow be blamed by fellow classmates for 'taking down' one of the most well-liked students at their school. She was painfully aware that kids could often be unfair in that way.

"Well, that was an experience," she heard as she stood looking down at the jewelry case below her. She was met with the soft green eyes of the customer who had come to her rescue earlier in the day.

"I'm James Wright," he said as he offered his hand from across the counter.

"Oh! Yes, Mr. Wright – I've been meaning to come and thank you once everything settled down. I really appreciate you stepping in like that," she said, shaking his hand.

"Please, call me Jim. And it was no trouble at all. I just hope those boys learned a lesson today they won't soon be forgetting."

"Yes, sir. I agree. I actually go to school with them," she said, glancing down at her shoes.

"I see," he said, seemingly understanding her concern. "Well, just know you handled it well. You'll come across people like that your whole life – it's just how you deal with them that counts."

June smiled. She didn't think there was anything that could have been said to make her feel better in that moment, but yet his words somehow helped. It was then that Edward made his way over to them, having just finished up with the last officer still remaining in the shop.

"Thank you for all your help today, sir," Edward said, offering his outstretched hand.

June and her father learned that Jim and his wife had recently moved into an older home not far from Randolphs. Edward swelled with pride as their new customer complimented the shop.

"We were happy to learn that the town was home to a fine jewelry store. My bride is a connoisseur of sorts," Jim said with a grin.

June stood quietly as her father proceeded to get into a detailed history of the shop, though she'd heard it all many times.

"Well, I think I'm in need of a break," Edward said, pulling his phone from his pocket. "Jim, I'd like to buy you a cup of coffee if you've got the time. There's a nice place just across the street."

"Sure, sounds good. I've been meaning to stop by there."

"June Bug, how 'bout you? I can call your mom and have her come down to keep an eye on the shop."

They hadn't had any new customers for a while, likely deterred by all the police cars out front, June thought.

"Yes, I'd like that. Instead of coffee, though, I think I'll order a milkshake," she said with a grin.

It was then that she suddenly recalled Jim's abrupt departure from the day before. *What could that have had to do with Mom?*

Though as her mother made her appearance downstairs several minutes later, June failed to detect a hint of recognition from either of them as introductions were made.

"Well, we'll be back in a bit, sweetheart," Edward said as they made their way out the door. Lorraine nodded as she made herself comfortable on a nearby barstool and grabbed one of her favorite magazines.

Once situated at the café, June was able to sit back and enjoy her milkshake as the two men interacted as though they'd known each other for years. Despite the fact that Mr. Wright was a good bit older than her father, they seemed to have a lot in common. She was happy to see him socializing with someone outside of work for a change. Though she and her parents attended a weekly church service, most of their free time was spent at home, per her mother's preference.

"So, young lady, how long have you been working at your daddy's shop?" Jim inquired as he took a sip of coffee.

"For as long as I can remember, really."

"My girl, here, is a great worker, Jim," Edward said, beaming at his daughter.

"Mr. Wright, I'm glad you came to see us again. To be honest, I was worried we'd made a bad impression on you yesterday," she said as she placed her hand on her father's shoulder.

"Please, call me Jim," he said with a grin. "I meant to apologize for being so short with you yesterday. I thought I saw someone in the shop that I knew from a long time ago, but I was mistaken."

"Oh, it was no problem at all. I hope you'll come back and see us again. It's always nice to get new faces around here," she said, taking another swig of her milkshake.

"I'd love to bring my wife, Roxanne, in to see the shop tomorrow if we find the time. I know she'd enjoy meeting you, as well, June."

"Great!" Edward replied enthusiastically. "I take care of my best customers – don't you worry about that."

Jim nodded as he finished off the last of his drink. "Well, I look forward to seeing you both again. Thanks again for the coffee." At this, he stood as they all offered their final goodbyes.

June and her father remained at the café a while longer, as she still had not made it to the bottom of her oversized milkshake.

"You did well today, Bug." Edward said as he patted his daughter's hand. "I know that couldn't have been easy – you knowing them and all."

"Thanks, Dad. Whatever comes my way after everyone gets word of this – I can handle it."

The pair took their time at the café. Though they mostly sat in silence, it was a break they both knew they desperately needed.

CHAPTER FOUR

June sat at the kitchen table later that evening – staring intently at her plate which was filled with orange chicken and fried rice. She listened as her father relayed the day's events to her mother, who was uncharacteristically hanging on his every word.

"So, what will happen to the Morris boy?" Lorraine asked.

"I don't know for sure. Figure I'll hear something in the next few days," he said as he helped himself to a second serving of orange chicken. "I am proud of our girl for catching it like she did." His wife nodded in agreement.

"I wonder if his mother will show her face at Bunco next week," Lorraine said, giving her husband a knowing glance. "June, how well do you know… what's his name? Ethan?"

"Not that well."

"I guess we'll see if anything's said about it on Facebook in the next few days. I hope no one tries to shift blame on us for calling the police. They may be kids but that was a $7,000 ring!" Lorraine exclaimed, looking to her husband for agreement.

"Absolutely. If I let it go this time, what would that say to every other heathen in town looking for a thrill?" Edward said, looking up at his daughter, who had still failed to touch her dinner. "None of this is your fault, June."

"Well, of course it's not. What should she have to worry about?" Lorraine asked, failing to notice her daughter's concerned expression.

"I know, sweetheart, but this might be tough for her – especially once school starts."

She knew that her father could not force Lorraine to understand her worries, but she was accustomed to receiving little to no validation from her mother. After taking a few bites of chicken, she helped her parents clean up before retreating to her room for the evening.

The next day, June wondered if the police would be calling with any news of the almost-robbery. She wasn't quite sure what to hope for as punishment for her classmates – *community service? Probation? Could they do jail time?* As she vacuumed the floors of the shop, she couldn't help but feel sympathetic when it came to the boys' parents. *They probably didn't raise them that way. I'm sure they are so embarrassed.*

It was then that she went in search of her father, whom she found sitting near the back of the shop, meticulously cleaning various pieces of jewelry.

"I'll go ahead and unlock the doors. We're at about three minutes 'til," she said.

"Sounds good, girl," her father replied, never once shifting his eyes from the piece he held between his thumb and index finger.

Making her way to the front, she remembered her promise to work on ideas for a new summer-themed window display. She felt at a loss as to how to make her father's vision a reality. As she sat on a nearby barstool to consider the complexities of making a giant sun which could be hung from the ceiling, the door of the shop opened to reveal her first customers of the day.

June's eyes met that of a woman who appeared to be in her late-fifties. She was impeccably dressed, though her clothes were a bit more flamboyant than June was accustomed to seeing on women of a certain age. She wore high-waisted, lime green pants in a fabric similar to silk. The pants were fastened with a belt which donned a large belt buckle. Her purple blouse was fashionably buttoned to the top. The large jewels she wore around her neck coordinated perfectly with the colors of her outfit. Her purple heels were at least six inches high, making it difficult to gauge her actual height. Though she wore a fair amount of makeup, she was undeniably beautiful. Her blonde hair was swept up gracefully in a bun atop her head, accented with a rhinestone barrette.

The woman smiled at June, who was still sitting on a barstool behind the jewelry counter. A man had entered the shop just behind the well-dressed woman, a fact of which June was only vaguely aware. She found herself a bit taken aback by the woman's chic style and striking good looks.

A familiar voice then broke the silence – "How are you this morning?" She hadn't realized until then that it was Jim Wright who had arrived with the woman.

"Good morning Mr. Wri... Jim. I'm doing well. How about you?" June asked as she stood to greet the couple.

"Oh, can't complain. The heat isn't quite as stifling today as its been. I'd like you to meet my wife, Roxanne," Jim said, placing his hand on his wife's back.

"Please, call me Roxie!" she exclaimed. She then threw her arms around June, despite the fact that they were still on opposite sides of the counter. "Jim has told me so much about you, sweetie. It's so nice to meet you!" Roxanne said as she released June from her warm embrace.

"It's nice to meet you, too. Your husband was a big help to us yesterday."

"Oh, yes, he told me all about those boys with the phony ring. What a sharp girl you must be! Brains and beauty – guess you've got it all, baby," Roxanne said as she lovingly patted June's hand.

She couldn't help but notice how well the couple complimented each other, as Jim was a bit more laid back. He let his wife do most of the talking, which Roxanne seemed to enjoy. She asked June about her summers spent working at the shop, as well as her plans for after graduation. Though she had never thought of herself as being particularly intriguing, Roxanne seemed genuinely interested in getting to know her.

"You and your father have such a beautiful shop here, and I've seen my fair share," she said as she browsed each of the glass counters.

"Thank you. I told my dad I'd work on ideas for updating the front window display, but I'm kind of drawing a blank."

"Oh, well I've dabbled in some interior design. You just let me know if I can help!" Roxanne said as she headed to the front of the shop to take a closer look at their current display.

June glanced at a nearby clock, realizing she had spent over thirty minutes talking to the Wrights. She found herself thoroughly enjoying the attention and compliments Mrs. Wright seemed to so freely give. She had never been one to need a lot of affirmation, but Roxanne's motherly-nature was undeniably a welcome addition to June's otherwise mundane work day.

"I love your Converse sneakers, dear. Not everyone can pull off the high-tops, but with your long legs they are adorable!"

"Thank you. I found them at my favorite clothing store down the street," June said, looking down at her feet.

"Yes! I've been meaning to stop by that boutique since we moved here. What is it called? Mathilde's?"

"Oh… yes, Mathilde's Boutique and Salon is just down the street as well. I… I actually meant the secondhand store is where I like to shop for clothes and shoes. The owner is always saving things for me."

"I see. Well you have beautiful taste," Roxanne said, smiling.

"Where's the boss man this morning?" Jim interjected.

"Oh! He's in his office – probably doing paperwork," she said, realizing she should have offered to let him know they were there so that introductions could be made. "Let me check to see if he's busy."

Edward emerged a few minutes later, following his daughter. "Well, good to see you again, Jim," Edward said as he made his way over to the couple.

"Good to see you, as well. My wife, Roxie, here has been eager to meet you, and to take a look around your shop. She's a bit of a jewelry collector herself," Jim said as he flashed his wife a grin.

"Mr. Randolph, you have yourself a fine establishment here," Roxanne said as she and Edward shook hands. "I must say, though, I'm even more impressed by your daughter. You and your wife must be very proud."

"Well I sure appreciate that, Roxie. She's a good egg," Edward responded, giving June a gentle pat on the back.

"Well now, I think I'd like to try on a few things. June, darling, would you mind showing me some of those necklaces?" Roxanne asked as she pointed at a nearby counter.

"Sounds great."

"Let's leave the boys to chat while we girls have some fun," Roxanne said as June grabbed her shop keys and made her way over to the necklaces.

It didn't take long for Roxanne to find several pieces she 'couldn't live without.' June enjoyed picking out styles for her to try, as her taste varied. She liked both antique pieces, as well as more modern designs. She seemed to gravitate toward bright, bold colors, but yet also picked out a few simple gold pieces.

June couldn't help but admire both her personal style and flamboyant taste. Though a mature woman, she was the very definition of a 'trend-setter,' June thought, glancing down at her own attire.

"Do you work on commission, dear?" Roxanne asked as she looked in a nearby mirror, admiring the sapphire necklace hanging around her neck.

"Um… well, yes ma'am. My dad pays me weekly, but I do also get a commission on my sales." June was fairly certain she had never been asked that question before.

"I'm glad to hear it," Mrs. Wright said with a wink. "Let's go check me out before I can do anymore damage."

The two ladies carefully laid out all of Roxanne's newest accessories on the counter. As June began to tally up the total, she noticed for the first time the rings that Mrs. Wright wore on her left hand. Her ring finger donned one of the largest diamonds she had ever seen in person – five or six carats at least resting upon a simple yellow gold band. She also sported several bands on both her ring finger, as well as her middle and index fingers. The bands varied in style and color, including stones such as rubies, morganites, and blue topaz.

"Your wedding ring is beautiful, Mrs. Wright... I love the bands, too. The combinations are so unique," she remarked.

"Please, dear, Mrs. Wright was my mother-in-law," she said with a grin.

"Oh, yes, I'm sorry... Roxie."

"You don't need to apologize, sweetie. I've always loved the look of stacked bands, don't you?"

"Yes, very much," she replied as she rang up the last of Roxie's haul. "I can offer you a 15% discount today. Dad always likes to take care of our best customers."

"Well I surely appreciate that, dear," Roxanne said as she motioned her husband over.

June was a bit surprised that Mr. Wright seemed completely unfazed upon learning the total cost for his wife's new jewelry.

"You know, I'm planning on stopping by the craft store if you'd like some help with the window display, June," Roxanne said as Jim gathered her bags.

"Oh, well... if it's not an inconvenience for you. That would be great," she responded, looking to her father for approval.

"You're too kind. I'm sure she would love the help," Edward interjected. "I'll take care of things here. Looking forward to seeing what you come up with, Bug."

June grabbed her crossbody purse from behind the counter before heading out the front door behind

Mr. and Mrs. Wright. Though she hadn't been looking forward to getting started on the window display, the idea of a midday outing was undeniably appealing. She also found herself enjoying her time spent talking to Mrs. Wright.

"How about I drop you ladies off at the craft store and I'll head to that kitchen place just a couple blocks down? I've been needing a few things for my grill," Jim said as they made their way outside.

"Jim does most of the cooking around our house. I do a lot of ordering out," Roxanne said, looking over at June. "That'll be fine, dear. Does that work for you, sweetie? We'll of course give you a ride back once we're done. No need for us to be out in the heat too long."

"Yes, that will be great."

As they made their way down the sidewalk, June noticed a vehicle parked on the side of the street which seemed out of place. It was a black car – a brand new Rolls-Royce. Jim retrieved his keys from his pocket before making his way over to the car. Though she had assumed the Wrights were somewhat well-off, she had never seen anything like this vehicle. She found it surprising that a couple of such means would have moved to their small town.

Jim opened the passenger-side door for his wife before moving on to the rear door for June. As she hopped in, she looked around in awe of the magnificence of her current ride. She had been driving a Honda Civic since she turned sixteen. It was twelve years old, and being a base model didn't exactly have a lot of 'bells and whistles.' Nevertheless, it was a reliable car, for which she was grateful.

As they drove the few blocks to the craft store, Roxanne chatted away, asking all about the town as they passed the shops lined along the streets.

"What made you decide to move here?" June asked.

"Well, dear, we just needed a change. Jim decided to retire early, and we had always wanted to get out of the city," she said, pointing out the craft store, insuring Jim wouldn't miss their stop.

"Well, ladies, I won't be far. Should be back in about thirty minutes, but if you finish up before that just shoot me a text," Jim said as he pulled up next to the sidewalk.

"Sounds good, honey," Roxanne said, gathering her purse and phone.

As they entered the store, Roxanne grabbed a nearby cart and started making her way down the aisles. She seemed very excited at the idea of helping out with the project. She threw out a lot of different ideas as they browsed, for which June was very grateful.

It wasn't long before they had a cart full of supplies, as well as detailed plans for the shop window. June was amazed at Roxanne's energy. She clearly knew what she was doing in the area of design. Not only had she worked out a plan for the giant, hanging sun Edward had requested, but she had also come up with ideas for the remainder of the window.

"Do you need any money, dear? I'd be happy to pay for this," Roxanne said, pulling out her wallet.

"Oh, no thank you!" June insisted. "I have my dad's card for shop expenses. I really appreciate all of your help – Dad will be thrilled."

"Well I enjoyed it!" she said, putting her wallet away.

As they placed their load of supplies onto the checkout counter, June noticed a woman as she made her way into the store. She sported short red hair and appeared to be June's mother's age – early forties maybe. Though the woman looked familiar, she was unable to place her.

Once again, she focused her attention onto emptying the cart in front of her. The man working checkout had already started scanning items and placing them in bags before she could get everything onto the counter, as she was running out of space. It was then that the silence was suddenly broken, like the horn of a train in the dead of night.

"Do you have nothing to say to me!?"

June turned to see the red-headed woman standing mere feet from her. She kept her eyes fixated on June, never even glancing at a stunned Mrs. Wright, nor the cashier.

"Umm… I don't… are you talking to me?" June asked nervously.

"Yes. I'm Stephen's mother," she said.

June suddenly realized how she knew the woman. Stephen Rains was a classmate, and coincidentally was one of the boys who had been involved in the incident at Randolphs the day before.

"My son and his friends could be facing serious charges. Do you know what that could do to his scholarship offers? It was nothing but childish antics… and now because of you and your father he could be in a lot of trouble! You couldn't have done the decent thing and just called us!?"

As she spoke, Mrs. Rains steadily raised her voice to an uncomfortably high volume. Her face looked flushed. Her hands were clenched tightly at her sides.

June then opened her mouth to speak, only to have it drowned out by an even louder voice than that of Mrs. Rains – it was Mrs. Wright.

"Now you listen here – the 'decent thing' to do would have been for you to raise your son not to be a criminal! Those boys are more than capable of taking responsibility for their actions," Roxanne said to a stone-faced Mrs. Rains. "Sounds like some discipline will be good for your son as he's clearly not getting any at home! Now you just turn yourself around and head out that door. You have no right to speak to a young lady like that!"

Mrs. Rains stood staring at Mrs. Wright; her body motionless. Her eyes grew wide, and her mouth began to quiver uncontrollably. After what seemed like an eternity, she turned and hastily exited the store without another word.

CHAPTER FIVE

June felt as though in a daze as she gazed down at the book which rested atop her lap. She had pushed her favorite chair into a corner of her bedroom, hoping to access the light of a nearby floor lamp. Though she'd been sitting there nearly an hour, she had yet to read a single word. Her body felt somehow weighted down by the day. The words of Stephen's mother still pierced her ears, though hours had passed since the encounter.

Upon her return to the shop earlier in the day, she had relayed details of the confrontation at the craft store to her father. Though clearly shaken by the news, Edward had done his best to comfort her by echoing similar sentiments as those of Mrs. Wright.

"I sure hate that for you. If she had something she needed to say, it should have been to me… you're just a kid," he said, shaking his head.

Though logically Mrs. Rains was clearly in the wrong, June was grateful for the validation. Her mother, on the other hand, wasn't quite as thoughtful in her response. Lorraine wasted no time in expressing her grievances via a Facebook post, which made very little effort in masking the situation to which she was referring. June couldn't help but wonder if Lorraine's anger was in response to Mrs. Rains' treatment of her, or if it was merely out of concern for her own reputation. As she sat, staring blankly at her bedroom door, she could hear as her mother vented in the living room.

"So, everyone thinks you should have just called their parents and not the police?" Lorraine asked loudly.

June could hear every word as her father tried in vain to calm his wife. "I'm sure it's not everyone, Lorraine. This was just one upset mother."

As she lay her head back, feeling the comfort of her tufted chair at the base of her neck, June became aware that her eyes had suddenly grown heavy. She could feel the weight of the book she held in her hands, yet had failed to read. Deciding to give in to the exhaustion, she could still hear her mother's voice just down the hall.

"That woman has a lot of nerve. I've got half a mind to call her…" she heard her mother say before drifting off to sleep.

The next day, she made a point to keep herself busy. Though she typically preferred helping customers over tasks such as pricing and cataloging new inventory, she suddenly found such work to be a welcome distraction. As she sat, meticulously pricing their new stock of engagement rings, she barely noticed that Mrs. Wright had entered the shop.

"Good morning, dear," Mrs. Wright said, beaming down at June.

"Oh! How are you, Mrs. Wri… Roxie? I didn't hear you come in," she replied as she stood from her chair, a bit dizzy from the sudden break in concentration.

"I just thought I'd stop by to see if you needed any help with the window display, sweetheart. I also want to check out that little boutique today."

"Well, I haven't had a chance to start on it yet... as I'm sure you can tell," she said, gesturing to the bare window. "I did clear it out this morning so that I could give the area a good cleaning before adding anything new... then I just got caught up with inventory."

"Then we've got a blank canvas to work with... perfect!" Mrs. Wright said as she zipped up her purse and placed it behind the counter.

"Okay, great. I'll go get our stuff," June replied, gathering up her books.

After laying out all of the materials they had purchased the day before, she and Mrs. Wright were hard at work. June finished cleaning up the space as Roxanne finalized her design for the window.

Edward meanwhile was hard at work helping customers, giving June the opportunity to focus solely on the task at hand. The pair hardly noticed when anyone entered the shop. She found herself thoroughly impressed with Mrs. Wright, particularly her leadership and organizational skills.

Neither of them had thought to check the time since starting their project. It wasn't until Edward mentioned lunch that they decided to take a break.

"Can I take you to eat? What do you like that's close?" Roxanne asked.

"That would be great! The café has good lunch specials if you think you might like that," she said, looking to her father for approval.

"That's very nice of you, Roxie. You ladies go on ahead and I'll hold down things here. I'll have your mom bring me something from upstairs in a bit," Edward said.

Once seated at the café, the pair wasted no time in discussing the progress they had made on the window display. Though she originally struggled to get excited about the project, June found herself undeniably invested. Mrs. Wright's enthusiasm was contagious, and her energy was something which June had never before encountered.

"I hope you weren't too upset after all that unpleasantness at the craft store yesterday," Mrs. Wright said before taking a sip of her tea. Though June was a little taken aback by the sudden change in subject, she knew the confrontation with Mrs. Rains was bound to come up eventually.

"Oh, that… I meant to thank you again for stepping in the way you did. I wasn't exactly expecting that yesterday… but I'm doing fine," June replied. She tried to smile, but found it difficult to muster. She had never quite developed the necessary skills for faking emotion. Edward always said she 'wore her heart on her sleeve.' She wanted desperately for what she was saying to be true – she wanted to be 'fine.' However, being publicly scolded by a classmate's mother had taken an undeniable toll on her.

"Sweetie, none of this is your fault. You and your daddy did the right thing. Those boys have a lot of growing up to do, and I think it started about the time the police showed up that day," Mrs. Wright said as she patted June's hand.

"I know. I just hate that I have to be involved at all... and my mother doesn't get it. She doesn't know what it will be like for me once school starts back. All she cares about is how it makes her look." As the words left her mouth, she could feel the pressure building behind her eyes. Her cheeks grew warm as she took a bite of casserole, trying in vain to keep the tears at bay. Mrs. Wright dug around in her purse for a few seconds before pulling out an embroidered handkerchief to offer her.

"I understand. And I'm here," Mrs. Wright said as June gave into the tears.

As the pair finished up their meal, they discussed details of the encounter with Mrs. Rains, as well as the initial incident with the boys. June did most of the talking as Mrs. Wright listened intently. Whether her worries be rational or irrational, she couldn't help but notice the care and concern with which Roxanne treated everything she had to say. It was nice, she thought, to say something out loud to another woman and have it matter to her.

"Say, how about we stop by Mathilde's before you head back to work?" Mrs. Wright asked as she signed for the bill.

"Well… I'd love to, but I don't want to leave my dad without any help for too long."

"Oh, I'm sure he won't mind – you deserve to have some fun."

"Yes, I'm… I'm sure he won't mind, but…," June began, a bit uncomfortable at the idea of imposing further.

"A purchase a day keeps the wrinkles away! You're too pretty to want for anything," Mrs. Wright said, standing from her seat and offering her hand.

"Okay, sure. It sounds like fun," June replied. "I'd love to help you shop."

Roxanne smiled as June stood from her seat, but said nothing in response.

As the pair entered Mathilde's, they were welcomed by the sweet aroma of perfume – the expensive kind, June thought. It had been a while since she had seen the inside of the boutique, and noticed the layout of clothing had changed a bit. They seemed to have added more racks of clothes, as well as displays of accessories such as costume jewelry, hats, and shoes. The salon portion looked to be the same as she remembered. Located in the back, it donned several stations which were currently full of clients having their hair tended to by attractive beauticians.

Mrs. Wright wasted no time in heading straight for the racks of clothing, which included a new summer collection – as noted by a chalkboard sign placed in a corner of the room. She noticed Roxanne filling her arms with clothing as she made her way through the store. June decided to take a look at the accessories – *there may be something I can find on sale.*

"See anything you like?" Mrs. Wright asked as June was trying on a pair of sandals.

"I do like these. I was thinking they might be nice to have since it's been so hot lately."

"Yes – I love those!"

"It seems like you found a lot! Are you going to try those on?" June asked.

"No, dear, *you* are. I just found a few things I thought you might like."

"Me? Oh… I really appreciate you looking for me, but I think I'll just stick with the sandals for today."

"Nonsense! Don't worry about the cost – everything is on me. You're my new pet, June Bug!"

She felt immediately embarrassed at the idea of Mrs. Wright buying her clothes. She had never before experienced so much attention, and wasn't sure how to respond. *How can I tell her no? Would that hurt her feelings? Mom wouldn't like it.*

"Thank you so much, Roxie… but I don't think I can let you do that," she replied tentatively.

Roxanne smiled as she placed the clothes on hooks inside a nearby changing room. "I won't take 'no' for an answer. I promise, it's no trouble at all."

As she felt unable to argue further, June reluctantly entered the changing room. The clothes Mrs. Wright had chosen were just June's style (albeit a bit more of her 'fantasy' style than an everyday wardrobe), and not one of them on sale. As she pulled back the curtain to show off each outfit to an excited Mrs. Wright, she couldn't help but feel a bit giddy herself.

It was exciting – trying on new clothes. As she checked herself out in a nearby full-length mirror, she felt good about her appearance. The clothes were not merely about practicality, as was most of her current wardrobe. They showed off her figure, while still being modest. They accentuated her features rather than masking them.

"You look so beautiful, dear. I think you should get it all," Mrs. Wright said as June tried on the final outfit from the pile of clothing in her changing room. "Well, now. Let's match up some of this jewelry with your new outfits."

June smiled, knowing it wouldn't do any good to contest – though she could feel her face growing warmer by the minute.

"That looks great on you," she heard as she and Mrs. Wright were looking over the display of necklaces. It was an employee of the boutique, whom June recognized from around town. She was small in stature – though her teased, blonde hair provided a few more inches to her height.

"Can I help you ladies with anything? I'm sorry I couldn't get here sooner; I was caught up on the phone," the woman said as she made her way over to them.

"That's no problem. We were just looking for some accessories to go with these outfits," Mrs. Wright replied, holding up a light blue, jeweled necklace to June, which contrasted perfectly with the navy dress she was wearing.

As the woman complimented their selections, June wondered what it must be like to have the time and money to dress like Mrs. Wright every day. She stood in awe as her new friend matched each of the outfits with various accessories, seemingly without batting an eye. She never even saw her glance at a price tag.

Mrs. Wright chatted away with the saleswoman, who was also impeccably dressed, wearing a yellow, knee-length summer dress with coordinating flats. The two women tried to include her in their choices, but June knew she was out of her league, to say the least. It wasn't long before they had an impressive collection of necklaces, earrings, hats, and shoes to go with her new wardrobe. As Mrs. Wright started piling everything onto the checkout counter, June looked down only to realize she was still wearing the navy dress, which was the last item she'd tried on.

"I forgot to change back into my own clothes," she said as she started to make her way back to the changing room.

"Oh no, dear. You don't need to change. We'll just put your old clothes in a bag, and then you can wear your new dress back to work – just let me grab the tag," Mrs. Wright replied.

"Umm… sure. That'd be great."

June wasn't entirely sure why she felt a bit apprehensive to wear the dress back to work. While she was excited about her new purchases, she began to wonder how her parents may react to the wardrobe… and the fact that she wasn't the one to pay for them.

As the saleswoman tallied everything up, June casually made her way over to a nicely-dressed mannequin. Trying to appear as though preoccupied, she thought it rude to stand next to Mrs. Wright as she paid for the haul of clothing and accessories. She also knew that if she were made aware of the total cost, it'd be difficult to move past the embarrassment. There was no turning back now. She knew any effort to talk Mrs. Wright out of making the purchase would be fruitless.

"I don't know how to thank you, Roxie. You're so generous," June said as they made their way back to Randolphs, shopping bags in tow.

"You're very welcome. You know I never had a daughter… this was probably more fun for me than it was for you!"

June felt as though she was finally starting to figure out Mrs. Wright. She and her husband were new to town, and with no children to keep up with… *maybe she's lonely*. She couldn't help but admit to herself that she was similarly happy to have the female companionship. Since school had let out for summer, she'd had very little social interaction, and her mother wasn't of any use in this area.

As they made their way back to the shop, Roxanne handed over the shopping bags she had been carrying. "I think it's time for me to head home to check on Mr. Wright. I really enjoyed my time with you today… how about I stop back by in the morning so we can finish up that display?"

"Yes, that sounds great. Thank you again for everything, Roxie. You're kind of the best," she replied with a grin.

At this, Roxanne pulled her in for a hug, the likes of which she was not used to receiving. June's mother was not very affectionate… and though a bit unexpected, she felt herself slowly ease into the embrace. Even if just for a few moments, she felt as though all the stress and anxiety she'd been carrying had disappeared. "I'll see you tomorrow," Roxanne said, pulling away. June watched as she made her way to her Rolls-Royce, which was currently being admired by several pedestrians along the sidewalk.

Later that evening, June stood in front of her closet, admiring her newly acquired garments. Necklaces draped around the necks of hangers, and earrings lay in small plastic baggies which June had fashioned with a slit near the top, so as to allow them to be hung with their corresponding outfit. Her new shoes carefully lined the floor of her closet, while her white Converse sneakers had been shoved to a back corner.

Though obligated to tell her father about her and Mrs. Wright's shopping excursion upon her arrival back at the shop, she'd managed to avoid seeing Lorraine for the time being. Her mother had been preoccupied with rearranging her curio cabinet to accommodate for her newest piece of Fenton for the majority of the evening. Though Edward was a bit taken aback by the thought of a near-stranger making such a purchase for his daughter, he was mostly thrilled to hear of the day she'd had.

As she sat on the floor of her closet, trying on a pair of gladiator-style brown sandals, she heard the buzzing of her cell phone which lay atop the lid of a nearby shoebox. Glancing at the screen as she continued to lace her sandals, she could see that she had a text from Reagan, one of the only girls from school June considered herself to be relatively close with. Reagan had left with her family for their condo in Florida just two days after school let out, as they did every summer.

Picking up the phone, June read the words, "Call me. I was just on Facebook. Did you know you're in the news!?"

CHAPTER SIX

The next morning as she opened the shop, June tried to listen in as she heard the muffled sound of her mother's voice behind a closed door. Lorraine was up much earlier in the day than usual. She and Edward had been on and off the phone for some time, barricaded in his office as they dealt with the situation at hand. It had been a rough night for *everyone*. June found herself unable to fall asleep until at least three in the morning.

Her worst fears had been realized the previous evening, as she poured over a news article which several of her classmates had shared to their Facebook pages. She felt as though unable to move her body as she read the headline, "Arrest of local teens sparks criticism: How far is too far?" The article detailed the events which had occurred at the shop just days prior, though names of the accused were never mentioned. In fact, the only name specifically noted was that of her father, identifying him as the owner of Randolphs. The article referred to the incident several times using the term "prank" – a characterization in which Edward took particular issue.

June knew that calling the police on her classmates was not something her father had taken lightly. In his entire career as a jeweler, Edward had not received a single piece of negative press. He took pride in the perfect five-star reviews that Randolphs sported online, as well as the positive feedback he received from customers on a daily basis at the shop. While the latest news article concerning his business was not referencing anything having to do with the quality of his work, he saw it as an attack – an unfair and unjust attack on everything he had worked to build.

By the time her parents finally emerged from the office, she was desperate for an update.

"Dad, who did you talk to?" she asked, as Lorraine made herself comfortable in a nearby chair, coffee mug in hand.

"Oh, just that newspaper. In fact, I talked to a *bunch* of people over at the Bishop Press-Tribune… had to call 'bout five times before they took down my name and number to give to someone in charge. Been spinning my wheels with interns all morning," he said, hanging his head as he wiped down a nearby counter.

"Idiots! Every one of them!" Lorraine chimed in from behind her oversized coffee mug. "Fabricating facts… downplaying an attempted robbery as an adolescent prank… we'll see how they like it when we sue the pants off 'em!"

"Try to stay calm, dear. I'm sure they'll issue a retraction once I tell them exactly what happened… just wish they would have called here to begin with," he replied solemnly.

"Please!" Lorraine exclaimed, throwing her head back in dramatic fashion. "You know at least one of those boys' parents must know someone at the paper! They're trying to make you look like the bad guy."

Edward made himself busy by helping June
finish up her morning tasks, failing to respond to his
wife's comments. As the morning drug on in silence,
she wondered if Mrs. Wright would stop by to help
finish work on the window display, as she'd promised.

Despite the sleepless night, June was excited to
wear one of her new outfits for the day. She sported a
pale pink, high-waisted skirt, which rested just above
her kneecaps. She tucked in a casual white t-shirt with a
small yellow flower, embroidered delicately on the
breast pocket, which Mrs. Wright had paired with the
skirt. The sandals which she had chosen for herself
somehow perked her up as she glanced down at her
feet, walking around the empty shop. She had found
herself in a bit of a trance before the solitude was
suddenly broken by the voice of her mother, still sitting
with the coffee mug she had refilled more than once in
the past hour.

"*What* are you wearing?" Lorraine asked,
seemingly confused by her daughter's appearance.

She had wondered how long it would take for
her mother to notice her new clothing. With all the
commotion of the previous evening, as well as that
morning, Lorraine had seemed as though completely
oblivious.

"It's new. It's from Mathilde's," she responded,
nervously adjusting her shirt, which was already
perfectly tucked.

"Yes, I know. I saw the skirt the last time I was
in… you went shopping?"

"I did. Yesterday... uh, Mrs. Wright – she's the wife of the man who helped us out the other day until the police came. She took me shopping," she said, trying desperately to find her words.

June's mother looked her over from head to toe – her perfectly plucked eyebrows furrowed in an expression that could only be described as pure bewilderment. "She... took you shopping. As in, she bought you those clothes... *why*!?"

"I... I don't know, Mom. She's just a really nice lady. She and her husband just moved to town and they don't really know anyone."

Edward then chimed in from across the shop. "You asking about Jim and Roxie, Lorraine? Fine couple... fine couple. Roxie seems to have taken an interest in our June Bug. Fine lady... she sure has an eye for jewelry, too. Nearly bought out the shop the other day, didn't she June?"

"Yes... I think they'll be very loyal customers," she responded, glancing over at her mother, who had finally cracked the first hint of a smile.

"Okay... well, that's nice I guess," Lorraine responded, looking her daughter over once more before burying her face into her cell phone.

It was then that June noticed something – her mother's phone. The case was cracked. Though semi-usable, there was a distinct crack running down the back of the case, through the pink flowers and glitter. Lorraine had always been one to take pride in everything she owned. From her clothes and shoes, to even her collection of coffee mugs, she had often been characterized as a perfectionist. If she noticed a small chip in one of their dinner plates or bowls, it was time for it to be replaced.

"Mom… what happened to your phone?" she asked. The words had barely left her mouth before she immediately regretted asking. She felt fairly certain that the case had sustained damage after being hurled at the wall by Lorraine, following a rather heated conversation. While the person on the other side of that phone call remained unknown to June, she wondered what he – or she – could have said to provoke such a reaction.

June's mother slowly peeled her eyes away from the screen of her phone to look up at her daughter. She then turned the phone over, as if unaware of the damage to her case. After running her finger along the crack, Lorraine paused to take a sip of coffee.

"I have no idea. Looks like I need a new case," she answered.

Her response was very matter-of-fact, said in a way that left no room for discussion, nor further inquiry.

"Well… I did see that they carry phone cases at Mathilde's now. It's not a big selection, of course, but the ones I saw were nice. Maybe you could check there before having to drive out to the mall," June said, trying desperately to seem as agreeable and helpful as possible. She knew she had struck a chord with her mother, and was admittedly fearful of retaliation.

Quickly darting out of her mother's eyesight, she pondered the potential repercussions should she continue to question Lorraine. *She doesn't know I heard her conversation… no, she can't. She does know that I keep making her uncomfortable… She's going to find a way to stop me from asking questions before long. I'll just make myself scarce today… she'll like that.*

It wasn't long before June found herself so preoccupied with helping customers that her thoughts began to quiet. Despite the less-than-flattering news article, which Edward felt made them out to be "insensitive and humorless," it was business as usual. She and her father worked while Lorraine remained in her chair, scrolling through her phone while still holding onto her long-empty coffee mug.

It was just after lunchtime that a beaming Mrs. Wright came strolling through the front door of the shop, as though she didn't have a care in the world.

"Hello, darling! How beautiful you look this morning… I'd a thought I was lookin' at a young Audrey Hepburn – just so chic!" Mrs. Wright exclaimed as June made her way from behind the counter to greet her.

"Well, you have great taste, Roxie!"

Mrs. Wright placed her oversized purse behind the counter before pulling her young friend in for a hug.

"How was your evening, dear? Did you have fun getting your wardrobe organized? I've always loved the sight of new clothes all hanging beautifully in a row. The colors, the textures… it never gets old," she gushed.

"Oh, yes… I had a great night," June responded, attempting to think only of the time before she'd received Reagan's text informing her that Randolphs was being publicly slandered.

Seemingly picking up on the hesitation in her voice, Mrs. Wright probed further.

"Is… anything the matter, dear?"

"Well… it's just that we've been having a bit of a drama since last night. The Bishop Press came out with an article about the almost-robbery. Seems like everyone and their mom has seen it. It's all over social media. It… it wasn't exactly good press for the shop."

"Oh yes, I saw that too!" Mrs. Wright exclaimed. "Jim showed it to me last night. I wouldn't worry too much about that, dear. People are smarter than that… most of the time anyway. They'll see right through it. No one needs to be embarrassed except for those boys – and the parents that clearly raised them without any sense!"

June nodded before noticing that her mother had suddenly walked up just behind her, seemingly out of nowhere. Lorraine still had her cell phone in hand as she introduced herself to Mrs. Wright. June found herself a bit taken aback for a moment as her mother put away her phone in order to offer her hand. Lorraine was not one to ever greet customers, at least not if she could help it. The time she spent in the shop typically consisted of getting on Facebook and flipping through magazines.

"Mom, this is Mrs. Wright," she said nervously.

"I see," Lorraine responded, carefully looking over the woman standing in front of her.

Mrs. Wright was dressed in a beautiful summer frock, which sported a pattern of flowers around the bustline and at the ends of the sleeves. Her high-heels only added to the striking presence which she so clearly possessed. The diamonds around her neck sparkled as the two women exchanged pleasantries.

Though Lorraine had been pleased to hear that Mr. and Mrs. Wright had made such a dent in sales on their previous visit to the shop, she suspected that her mother wouldn't be too fond of her new friend. Mrs. Wright was just the kind of woman that Lorraine didn't care for – a woman she found intimidating.

By June's estimate, Mrs. Wright was at *least* fifteen years older than Lorraine. June knew that when weighed in the balance, Roxanne's good looks, charm, and expensive clothing would be too much for her mother to look past.

"So, I hear you and your husband just moved to town," Lorraine said, clearly trying her best to seem friendly.

"We did. And I must tell you, I've so enjoyed getting to know your daughter. She's a real gem... though I'm sure I don't need to tell *you* that!" Mrs. Wright said, winking at June.

"Well, I'm sure most any girl her age would enjoy a shopping trip to Mathilde's... I hope you'll allow us to reimburse you for the clothes," Lorraine said, increasingly abandoning her efforts to mask the discontentment in her voice.

"Oh, that's not necessary at all, my dear. I was happy to do it… and I'm sure Mr. Wright was just happy to have the house to himself for a bit while I had some girl time."

June could sense that her mother was becoming increasingly flustered. *Why does she care if Mrs. Wright wants to spend time with me? It's not like she does!* June stood in silence as she contemplated ways in which she might break the tension. Even as her mother continued to push the subject, Mrs. Wright remained cordial as ever.

"While we certainly appreciate your generosity, Mrs. Wright, I'm sure you understand that my husband and I can pay our own way when it comes to our child… and it would make us more comfortable to do so."

"Goodness me, dear, it seems you and your husband do a fine job caring for Miss. June here! I just wanted to give the girl a bit of a treat…," Mrs. Wright said before being cut off by the ringing of Lorraine's cell phone.

As her mother reached for the phone inside her pocket, June took an audible sigh of relief at the prospect of an end to the conversation.

"I… excuse me, I have to take this…," Lorraine managed to get out before quickly heading towards the stairs. Though curious as to why her mother needed to take the call in the privacy of their apartment, she was admittedly happy to see the back of her.

"I'm so sorry about that, Roxie. My mom is… well, she's not the best at expressing gratitude. I'm so thankful for everything you and Mr. Wright have done.

You've been so good to me," she said, her embarrassment quickly turning to feelings of anger toward her mother.

"Don't worry about a thing, sweetheart. I had a mother once too, you know? Now, how 'bout we get to work on that window?"

Though she was grateful for the kindness of Mrs. Wright, she found herself having a hard time letting go of the animosity she felt towards her mother, as a result of her blatant rudeness. Seemingly sensing her discontentment, Roxanne did her best to lift her spirits as they worked.

June hardly glanced at the clock as they chatted, putting all of the finishing touches on their display. Edward took the time to complement their efforts in the midst of helping customers.

"Well that window looks like it belongs in a magazine, ladies," he said just as they were cleaning up.

"Thanks, Dad. We were about to head outside to look it over one more time before calling it a day. I think it's finally finished."

The three made their way outside, with Edward continuing to shower them with praise, which June had to admit to herself was a welcome contrast to the recent interaction they'd had with her mother. She hoped that his friendliness would somehow make up for Lorraine. They all took a moment to gaze at the finished product before Mrs. Wright broke the silence.

"Well Mr. Randolph, I do believe you'll have more walk-in customers than you know what to do with. I know I'd have a hard time walking past this storefront without stopping in," she said as June's father beamed with pride.

"To tell ya the truth, Roxie, we may need it. Found out we had a bit of bad press yesterday."

"Yes, I heard… and it's like I told your girl earlier, I wouldn't lose any sleep over that. It'll keep being business as usual, I'm sure," Mrs. Wright said with a reassuring smile.

"Would you like something to drink, Roxie? We could head over to Mr. Haygood's stand for some lemonade," June suggested.

"Great idea, Bug, I'm sure Roxie here needs a minute to relax. We also have a pitcher of sweet tea upstairs… made it myself!" her father interjected.

"Oh, sweet tea sounds heavenly! Can I help you bring it down?"

"You just make yourself comfortable inside and I'll go get the pitcher," June said as they all made their way back into the shop.

She could hear her dad chatting away as she made her way up the steps to their apartment. Once again, June felt grateful that she had at least *one* parent she could count on to be gracious. Though she'd been distracted by the cheery personality of Mrs. Wright, she found herself once again feeling angry towards her mother as she began to recall their uncomfortable encounter earlier in the day. As she reached the apartment, she could find no trace of Lorraine, for which she was relieved. She wasn't ready to see her. She wasn't ready to pretend as though everything were fine, like she always had.

Making her way to the kitchen, she grabbed a package of disposable cups from the pantry before fetching the pitcher of tea. Just as she had balanced the stack of cups under her arm so that she would have one hand free, she noticed her mother's cell phone sitting on the kitchen table. She walked slowly back towards the door with every intention of heading downstairs.

It was *then* that her mother's unkind words to an innocent-Mrs. Wright began to replay in her mind. It was *then* that June began to consider the many years she had spent walking on eggshells and making excuses for her mother's cold demeanor. It was *then* that she considered the possibility that a perfect stranger's motherly nature appealed to her the way that it did because she lacked such a figure in her own life. It was *then* that June became irrationally – or perhaps rationally – angry at Lorraine in a way she had never before experienced.

She quietly scanned the apartment for any sign of her mother before walking over to the table and picking up Lorraine's cell phone, using her one free hand. Her eyes darted quickly from her mother's phone and back to the hallway. While she had no way of knowing how long she might have before Lorraine would emerge from her bedroom, she found herself hastily scanning through her recent phone calls. Perhaps hoping to find a name she didn't recognize – or any other clue as to the identity of her mother's mystery caller – June stopped cold as she saw the letters "P.I." appear on the screen.

CHAPTER SEVEN

June startled at the faint sound of bare feet hitting the hardwood floor in her mother's bedroom. She felt certain that once Lorraine realized she had left her phone out of sight she'd be making her way out of her room in search of it. After carefully placing the phone back on the table, she headed downstairs – the pitcher of tea in tow.

Mrs. Wright complimented Edward on his homemade sweet tea as she took a seat in a nearby chair. As June took a sip from her own cup, she couldn't help but wonder if Roxie was merely being polite. The sweetness of the tea rivaled that of a thick syrup – just like the Randolphs liked it. She doubted that their taste for it would be shared by many.

Though her mind was preoccupied, she did her best to keep up with the conversation between her father and Mrs. Wright. He seemed intrigued as Roxie relayed details of the renovation that their new home had undergone.

"Jim was insistent on a gourmet kitchen… I tell ya it was a task trying to oversee everything when we hadn't yet moved here," Roxie said. "Though it *was* nice to have everything turn-key once we arrived. No one wants to live in a construction zone."

"I can imagine," June's father said as he stood to greet an incoming customer. "Excuse me just a moment, ladies..."

"You know, dear, we also put in a pool. If you'd be interested in taking a break from this heat, we'd love to have you anytime. Jim and I have only used it a few times," Mrs. Wright said as she sipped her tea.

"That would be nice! I love to swim... though I wouldn't want to intrude on you," she replied.

"It would be our pleasure... we should have bought you a swimsuit yesterday! It sure didn't even cross my mind."

"Oh no, I have one. That's not a problem," she said, watching as her father was wrapping up with the customer he'd been helping.

"Wonderful. What day would be good for you?" asked a beaming Mrs. Wright. "Our calendar is pretty much wide open... that's what happens when you get to be our age, dear. Though I *am* glad Jim was able to retire when he did – we're still young enough to enjoy ourselves."

At this, Edward interjected as he made his way over from the cash register – "I haven't ever thought much about retirement, myself... though there will come a day I s'pose. Hoping Bug here might want to take over at some point."

"Well, you're still so young – bet you've got at least twenty years before you'd need to think about that," Mrs. Wright said thoughtfully.

"Lord willing, Roxie... Lord willing," he responded as he poured himself another glass of tea. "Sounds nice though, you and Jim getting out of the big city... enjoying time together. I can't seem to recall if you said you two got any kids?"

"We don't... it just never happened for us," she answered, smiling politely.

"Yeah, I hear ya," he said. Edward was never one to pry, and it seemed to June that he felt a bit uncomfortable in having asked the question.

"Though we *were* blessed in a lot of ways... Jim and I have spent over forty years together. We were high school sweethearts, ya know."

At this, June couldn't help but interject. "What a great story... no wonder you two are so in sync," she said with a grin.

"Yes, well, ya get to know a person after a while," Mrs. Wright replied. "Speaking of which, Edward - your girl and I were just talking about her maybe coming over to the house to check out the pool, if that's alright with you and the Mrs."

"Well that sounds like fun! We wouldn't mind in the least," he answered.

"Great! Would sometime this weekend work for you, June?"

"I'll be working tomorrow... but Sunday would be good," she replied.

At this, Edward interjected, "Oh don't worry 'bout that, Bug – if you want to go tomorrow, I'll be just fine holding down the fort here."

She could tell that her father desperately wanted her to have some fun. "Well, if you're sure, Dad – that'd be great."

"Wonderful! I'll be here in the morning to pick you up... how does ten o'clock work for you?" Mrs. Wright asked as she started to gather her things.

"Sounds great! See you then," June said as she found herself, almost instinctively, standing to give her new friend a hug goodbye.

Later that evening, June sat in front of her dresser – surrounded by a mountain of clothes which unfortunately did not contain the pale pink bathing suit she'd been searching for. Moving on to look through the cedar chest that sat at the foot of her bed, she heard footsteps belonging to none other than her mother as she made her way down the hall. As she opened the door, June wondered why she even bothered to knock if she wasn't willing to wait for a response.

"Why is it such a mess in here?" her mother asked haughtily.

"I'm trying to find my bathing suit," she replied, never taking her eyes off the contents of her cedar chest as she continued her search.

"You're... going swimming?"

"That's usually why people need a bathing suit, Mom."

She knew that she was taking a risk by being short with her mother, yet felt unable to mask her disdain. For her, Lorraine had crossed a line when she treated an innocent-Mrs. Wright so poorly earlier in the day. Apart from her father, Roxie was the first adult to show such a genuine interest in her in a very long time. It seemed to her that as the years passed, her mother had grown increasingly indifferent toward her.

"Uhh... you... and where are you planning on swimming?" she asked, clearly taken aback at her daughter's response.

"The Wright's house... Mrs. Wright is picking me up in the morning."

"Don't you have to work tomorrow?" Lorraine retorted. "Is that fair to leave your daddy without any help?"

"Maybe you could help out, Mom. What else do you have to do?"

Lorraine folded her arms and furrowed her brow as she made her way closer to where her daughter sat on the bedroom floor.

"As a matter of fact, I have a lot of errands to run tomorrow. You're not going anywhere on a Saturday," she said in a way that seemingly left no room for discussion.

Finally deciding to look up, June knew how badly she'd hit a nerve, as her mother's left eye began to twitch.

"Dad already said I could go... you can ask him. I don't even have her phone number to cancel," she responded, confident that this was one situation her mother would be unable to ruin.

It took Lorraine a while to respond, as she was clearly still in shock as to her daughter's newfound defiance.

"I'll talk to your dad about this. And get this room cleaned up!" she shouted before storming out.

Focusing her attention back to the stacks of clothing that lay neatly in her cedar chest, she couldn't help but feel okay about back-talking her mother. As she rifled through the clothes, she spotted her bathing suit under a stack of old Christmas sweaters (which had long been too tight on her). Though she was fairly certain the swimsuit would fit, as it was a bit loose on her small frame two years prior when Lorraine had passed it down, she decided to try it on.

Looking at herself in the full-length mirror which hung on her closet door, she felt relieved that the suit did indeed fit her tall, slender frame. It was a simple one-piece swimsuit – nothing special. There may have been a time when worn by her mother that the pink wasn't quite so pale, but it would certainly do.

As she slipped back into her shorts and oversized t-shirt, she recalled a time when she had been invited to a pool party in middle school. It was the birthday of none other than Ethan Morris. Ethan's parents had asked him to invite his entire class over to their house, as they had recently put in a massive inground swimming pool.

Though they had *never* been what she would consider to be friends, she couldn't recall having any negative feelings toward him at the time – merely indifference really. He wasn't yet the arrogant guy that he'd turned out to be once they made it to high school. Ethan had shot up about four inches during the summer between eighth-grade and freshman year. This resulted in a much slimmer figure for an increasingly-confident Ethan. By the time he'd been gifted a truck for his sixteenth birthday, all traces of the relatively pleasant boy she had known in middle school had all but disappeared.

Thinking back on the day of his party, June recalled that she had begrudgingly attended at the urging of her mother. It was the first pool party she had ever been invited to, and the prospect of wearing a swimsuit in front of most of their seventh-grade class was particularly daunting. Ethan's birthday fell on one of the last weekends in May, which happened to be the first weekend of summer break that year.

Sitting in front of her dresser, June began folding the clothes still scattered on the floor around her. She spotted a corner of her cell phone peeking out from under a pile of leggings. In the search for her swimsuit, she had been unaware that it was even misplaced.

She was surprised to see a text from her friend, Reagan, checking in to make sure she was okay. The article concerning the almost-robbery had continued to make the rounds on Facebook, though June was making a conscious effort to stay off social media for the time being. Responding to her text, she recalled that Reagan had also been in attendance at Ethan's seventh grade pool party.

She remembered looking at her bare legs and attempting to pull her swimsuit cover-up down as much as possible before arriving at Ethan's house. Her mother had driven her. She remained mostly quiet on the ride there, caught up in her own racing thoughts. She recalled the pain in the pit of her stomach at the thought of removing her cover-up in front of everyone. *Would it be weird if I just don't swim? My legs are so dry and pale... Maybe I could say I don't feel well.*

She could remember that car ride like it was yesterday. Even then she knew that it wouldn't do any good telling her mother how she was feeling – *she would never understand.* Pulling into Ethan's neighborhood, she felt relieved when she spotted a group of girls from her class standing outside the house, talking amongst themselves. *They're not swimming yet*, she thought... *It will be fine if I never get in the pool.*

She glanced over at her mother before gathering her beach towel from the floorboard.

"Your dad will be here to pick you up around eight."

"Okay... thanks for the ride, Mom," she said before mustering a polite smile as she exited the car.

She felt a bit silly for having been so worried – *this will be fine.* Making her way over to her classmates, she had a newfound confidence that she might actually enjoy herself. She even considered that maybe she'd been too hard on her mom for forcing her to go to the party. Maybe Lorraine genuinely thought she would have a good time. Walking along the driveway, she turned to wave goodbye to her mother as she was getting ready to pull away.

June could so easily recall the sensation of her ankle bending rapidly beneath her. She even remembered the taste of grass as she tried in vain to catch herself. Her beach towel and phone lay beside her as she slowly tried to gather herself, brushing dirt from her face, bare knees, and elbows. Ethan's driveway had a short drop off between the concrete and grass. A fact of which June was previously unaware before turning to wave goodbye to her mother, and subsequently losing her footing.

As June sat in her uncharacteristically messy bedroom, folding clothes and placing them neatly back in her dresser drawers, she could still hear the roar of laughter that came from the girls standing mere feet away from where she had fallen. She remembered not being able to look up. She couldn't. *What do I do now?* She remembered the pain – the fear.

Gathering up her towel and phone, she prayed that her mother was still there. She thought maybe she'd get out of the car to help her. Maybe this would create some sort of buffer between herself and the girls, making it somehow a little less uncomfortable.

Standing up, still brushing off the dirt and grass remnants that remained stuck to her kneecaps, she looked back. Her mother's car sat with the front bumper still in the driveway – the remainder in the street. June could see that her hand was covering her mouth, though it wasn't a look of concern in her eyes. She could see that Lorraine was making a very poor attempt to stifle her laughter.

Piling a stack of folded t-shirts into the bottom drawer of her dresser, she could still recall the profound emptiness that she experienced as that seventh grade girl. It was in that moment she knew Lorraine would never be the mother she wanted. Standing in front of Ethan's house, hastily refolding her faded beach towel as her hands shook from sheer humiliation – she was on her own.

Turning her full attention back to the task at hand, she quickly finished restocking her dresser before making her way over to her bed. *She'll let me go tomorrow, she has to… Dad will take care of it*, she thought as she folded her pillow in half and let her body sink into the mattress. It was then that she remembered Lorraine's apparent phone call with a private investigator. *That's the only thing 'P.I.' could mean, isn't it? There's no way this is something Dad knows about.*

She wondered if digging through her mother's Facebook page would yield any insight as to her need to speak to a private investigator. Though she didn't think it prudent to continue to probe her personally, she needed to know what her mother was hiding. Whether it was an inevitable result of the past several years of cold indifference that Lorraine had inflicted upon her, or merely a kneejerk reaction to her treatment of Mrs. Wright – June was angry. She felt unable, or perhaps merely unwilling to let it go.

Wanting to ensure that Lorraine hadn't convinced her father otherwise, she sprang from her bed to confirm that her plans with the Wrights were still on for the next day. She found Edward sitting in the living room watching TV – his feet rested at the end of his recliner.

"Dad, is it still okay for me to go with Mrs. Wright in the morning?"

"Sure. No problem, Bug. I bet you'll have yourself a good time. You got you a suit, don't ya?"

"Yes, I found one," she replied before plopping down on the couch.

"Did… Mom say anything to you about it?" she asked hesitantly.

"Oh yeah. She was just worried I'd be overwhelmed at the shop tomorrow, that's all. I told her I'd be just fine," he said, giving her a reassuring grin.

"Okay… thanks," she said, relieved that Lorraine had been unable to sway him.

"You know, kid… your mama – she's got the right intentions. She may not always have a way with words… I know that. I get it can be hard on you… but she means well."

"Yeah, I'm sure she means well," she replied, knowing nothing of the sort.

"You know, losing her own mom when she was just eighteen… she was just a bit older than you. As you've gotten older… well, I'm guessin' she might not quite know how to parent a girl your age. She just had to grow up so darn fast herself."

"Right… I get it, Dad. I do."

She then noticed a new piece of glass in her mother's curio cabinet. It looked a bit like a perfume bottle – donning an elaborate top and intricate pink flowers painted on both sides of the body.

"She buy some more Fenton?" June asked, trying to mask her annoyance at her mother's spending habits.

"Nah, that one there came in the mail from your grandfather yesterday."

"Huh… didn't she get something from him last week too?" she asked, recalling the FedEx package she'd seen on the kitchen counter just a few days prior.

"Yep, she did. It's kind of a strange deal… he's been sending her all kinds of stuff lately… things he knows she likes. But when he calls me askin' to speak to her she tells me to let him know she's busy. I'm not sure quite what to make of it myself," he replied, shrugging his shoulders and turning his attention back to the TV.

CHAPTER EIGHT

The next morning, June stared at her reflection as she wrestled with her long, tangled hair. In an attempt to recreate the perfect 'messy' bun, she could feel her frustration building. Though a pool day is widely considered a casual affair, she couldn't help but want to look nice for Mrs. Wright. Slipping into her swimsuit, she hoped Roxie wouldn't judge her for the suit's faded appearance. She chose to sport one of her new summer frocks as a cover-up – a flowy, green ombre dress that Mrs. Wright loved in the store. Pairing the dress with her new sandals, she was resolved to the fact that making yet another attempt to perfect the bun atop her head would fail to yield different results. *This is as good as it's gonna get*, she thought as she made her way to the laundry room in search of a bottle of sunscreen.

Her sensitive skin had been an issue for as far back as she could remember. While many of the girls in her class frequented the local tanning salon throughout the year, she found it necessary to saturate her skin in suntan lotion when planning to spend an extended period of time outdoors. Though her complexion was undeniably similar to that of her mother, she had always felt that Lorraine's darker hair offered a better contrast to their ultra-fair skin. Though she had never felt 'unattractive' per se, she couldn't help but hope that her looks might 'blossom' a bit in the future.

Stuffing the bottle of lotion into her bag, she walked to the kitchen where she found her father enjoying his morning coffee. Randolphs didn't open until ten o'clock on Saturday mornings, giving Edward a bit more time to sleep in. Playing cards lay spread across their kitchen table; the patriarch of the family sat enthralled in his weekly game of solitaire. Edward was undeniably a creature of habit – playing every Saturday, right up until it was time to open the shop.

"Who's winning?" she inquired cheekily.

"All I can tell ya is it's not me, darlin' – seems I'm having an off morning," he replied.

"Want me to help out downstairs until Mrs. Wright gets here?" she asked, taking a seat beside him.

"Nah, don't worry about that. I'll be heading down there in a few… you just have yourself some breakfast."

"Is Mom up yet?" she asked, hoping she wouldn't have to endure an awkward run-in.

"Not yet… your mama hasn't been sleeping too good the last few weeks. Then this business with that article sure hasn't helped," he replied, topping off his cup of coffee.

Though she couldn't imagine what Lorraine had to lose sleep about, she wondered if it had anything to do with the private investigator with whom she'd been communicating.

"I think I'll just have some coffee too – I'm really not very hungry," she said as she reached for her own mug.

It wasn't long before Edward decided it was time to head downstairs to get ready for the day. Since she wasn't expecting Mrs. Wright for another twenty minutes, June decided to take a seat in her father's recliner as she finished her coffee.

Staring at her mother's curio cabinet, she found herself appreciating the beauty of Lorraine's extensive collection of Fenton glass. The cabinet was always kept in immaculate condition, with not a hint of dust in sight. As she sat in the silence of their living room, she couldn't help but wonder if her mother could ever be as invested in their relationship as she was in her collection of glass.

At five minutes 'til, she gathered her things and made her way down to join her father as she awaited the arrival of Mrs. Wright. Randolphs was quiet as she headed over to their mini-fridge to grab a bottled water. She adjusted her glasses as they slipped slightly down the bridge of her nose. It was then that she heard a knock at the door. Roxanne Wright was beaming from ear to ear as she stood in front of the shop. As Edward hurriedly opened the door (which had become prone to sticking with age), the silence of the shop was immediately overtaken by the exuberant presence of Mrs. Wright.

"Good morning, Edward! Nice to see you on this fine Saturday," she said as she made her way inside.

"Mornin,' Roxie. Looks like you ladies picked yourselves a good day for swimming," he said, gesturing toward the front windows.

"Yes. Nothing but blue skies, Miss. June!" Mrs. Wright said, walking toward her young friend. "Did you happen to pack your sunscreen, or do we need to stop somewhere on the way?"

"Oh, no ma'am. I have plenty," she replied, placing her hand on the bag that hung on her shoulder.

"Well, none the less, you just let me know if that sun ever starts to get to you and we'll head on inside," Mrs. Wright said, smiling back at Edward who stood near the front door.

The pair made their way outside. Opening the passenger-side door of the Wrights' Rolls-Royce, which again attracted the attention of numerous passersby, June noticed a clear gift bag with pink tissue paper resting in the front seat.

"Umm… is it okay if I sit this in the back, Roxie?" she asked tentatively.

"That's for you, dear. Why don't you go ahead and open it?" Mrs. Wright replied, settling into the driver's seat.

The bag contained a beautiful one-piece swimsuit, along with coordinating headband. The color of the suit was a soft lavender with a navy gingham pattern. She found herself unable to speak as she sat staring at the vintage-inspired swimsuit, which she recognized as coming from Mathilde's Boutique.

"I don't understand, Mrs. Wright. I don't understand why you're so nice to me," she said, trying in vain to hold back tears.

"Oh, please don't cry, sweetheart – that's nothing. I just swung back by Mathilde's this morning 'cause I thought you might could use a new swimsuit," Roxanne said as she searched for tissues in her console.

"Thank you," June replied, wiping away tears. She hated that she couldn't contain her emotion. She was overwhelmed by the generosity of a woman she barely knew. Seemingly sensing that she didn't want to talk about it further, Mrs. Wright quickly changed the subject as she pulled out onto the street.

The home of Jim and Roxanne Wright was a short ten-minute drive from Randolphs. Upon pulling into the circular driveway, June was left stunned at the sheer size of the home. It was a two-story Colonial style estate. The massive lawn was manicured to perfection, donning dozens of rows of brightly colored hydrangeas.

She noticed a boy installing what appeared to be some sort of security camera near the front door. He looked to be about her age, sporting a basketball shirt that included the name and mascot of a neighboring high school. She didn't know much about the school, other than that it was private. He stood just north of six feet, with dark hair and olive-colored skin.

"Good morning, Luca!" Mrs. Wright exclaimed as they made their way toward the front of the home.

"Good morning, Mrs. Wri… Roxie," he responded, clearly having received the memo on how she preferred to be addressed.

"I want you to meet June Randolph – she's come to keep me company today," Roxie said with a smile.

"I'm Luca," he said, shaking her hand. She wasn't accustomed to kids her own age being so formal.

"Jim met Luca here at the hardware store and asked him if he'd come help us out this summer. He takes care of the yard and any other little odds and ends we need," Mrs. Wright explained, gesturing toward the security camera he was working on.

June learned that although Luca lived close by, he was able to attend his private school due to the fact that his mother currently taught English literature there. Like June, Luca would be starting his senior year in the fall. She couldn't help but wonder what it might be like to go to a different school, especially with the Ethan Morris incident hanging over her head.

Upon entering the front door, she was immediately taken by the beauty of the home. The family room donned a stunning white-brick fireplace with a grand mirror hanging above it. The white couches were accented with dozens of throw pillows, which offered beautiful pops of color and texture. The kitchen featured oversized, gray cabinetry with contrasting white granite for the spacious countertops. The stainless appliances were like nothing she had ever seen, clearly designed to accommodate gourmet-style cooking. The heavy drapery sported a chevron pattern in royal blue, which perfectly accented the light colored walls. The home struck a perfect balance of vintage-charm and modern touches. Lit candles were displayed atop several pieces of furniture throughout the first floor, permeating the air with pleasing scents.

"So, the family room, dining room, kitchen, and office are all down here... and all of the bedrooms are on the second floor, if you'd like to see upstairs next," Mrs. Wright said proudly. "Oh, and the bathroom is right over there, dear, if you'd like to change into your new suit once we've finished the tour."

As she and Roxie made their way up the stairs, she noticed the framed family photos that lined the wall. She paused for a moment to take a closer look at a wedding photo, which she quickly realized was that of a young Mr. and Mrs. Wright.

"Would you believe that was us? We were babies!" Roxie said, taking a closer look at the photo.

"How old were you there?" June asked.

"We were both twenty… nearly twenty-one. We wanted to get married right out of high-school, but our parents insisted we wait a bit."

The second floor featured five bedrooms and three additional bathrooms. The master bedroom alone appeared to be nearly the size of the Randolphs' entire apartment, June thought to herself as Mrs. Wright excitedly detailed the process of refinishing the home's original hardwood floors. Each bedroom donned grand, vintage furniture – the likes of which June had only seen in magazines or movies set in the time period. Mrs. Wright paused at the doorway of the final bedroom at the end of the hall. It had to be the most elaborate of them all, she thought as Roxie motioned for her to step inside.

The centerpiece of the room was an oversized, canopy bed with a pale pink comforter, and no less than four rows of throw pillows in varying sizes. A large vanity placed in a corner near the window sported what looked to be several bottles of expensive perfume. The wardrobe, which sat against the wall opposite the bed, featured curvature and design elements which could only be described as being fairytale-like. The walls were adorned with several original paintings – the most striking being a large, framed portrait of a young girl in a lace dress and pearl necklace, which hung above the bed.

"This room is so beautiful… they all are," June said as she made her way over to take a peek out of the window, which offered a view of the swimming pool and backyard. "How have you been able to do all of this so fast?"

"Well thank you, dear. Luca has helped us out a lot… but don't be fooled – we still have plenty of boxes in the garage just waitin' to be unpacked," she said with a slight smirk.

Mrs. Wright made her way back to the kitchen while June changed in the downstairs bathroom. The new suit fit perfectly – flattering her in a way that her hand-me-down swimsuit couldn't. As she looked at herself in the mirror, she couldn't help but feel a sense of confidence. It was not a feeling she was accustomed to.

Upon entering the kitchen, she was welcomed by the aroma of baked goods. Roxie was in the process of unloading several trays of food from the refrigerator. Tea cakes, croissants, muffins, and a variety of fruit lined the granite countertop.

"I didn't know what you might like so I bought a little of everything. I found the cutest little tea room while I was in town yesterday and had them put together some trays for us," Roxie said as she carefully placed a pitcher of orange juice next to the spread.

It was then that she heard the front door open, turning to see a beaming Mr. Wright walking towards them.

"Well hello again, June! I see you're about to try Roxie's famous cooking," he said cheekily.

"Oh, you hush… or you won't get any," Mrs. Wright replied with a grin.

The three sat around the kitchen table and chatted as June snacked on a cranberry-orange muffin.

"Oh, Jim – be sure to ask Luca if he would like some brunch. The child must be thirsty by now; he's been here all morning," Roxie said as her husband cleaned his plate of a second helping.

"I was just out there and he'd grabbed a water bottle from his truck. I'll check on him in a bit; I promise."

"Well was it in a cooler? He may need some ice; this heat is downright stifling," she retorted, heading toward the cabinet to fetch a glass.

Jim shrugged his shoulders as his wife made her way out of the kitchen, the glass of shredded ice in tow.

"My wife hears what she wants to hear and disregards the rest," Mr. Wright said, smiling. "Paul Simon said something along those lines."

June nodded as she instinctively started gathering plates and tidying up the kitchen table.

Though she wasn't sure *why*, she felt the need to keep herself busy while Mrs. Wright was away. It wasn't that she didn't *want* to talk to Jim, but he just couldn't match the reassuring presence of his wife.

"So, uhh… does your mama work at the jewelry shop much or just you and your daddy?" he asked, as June made her way back from the sink.

"Oh, well, she helps out some – it's not really her thing though. She takes care of our apartment… runs our errands."

"I see… I expect that takes up most of her time – taking care of the house and a kid. Not to say you're not almost grown."

"Yes, it keeps her busy enough… she has a beautiful collection of this glass – it's called 'Fenton.' She's very proud of it."

"Oh, yeah - Fenton. I'm very familiar with it. Do you enjoy collecting too?" he asked.

"No, no… I mean, I love it. But, she's very particular about it… which I understand."

"I see. She, uhh… keep a very close watch on you? I mean, would you say she's strict?"

"Umm… no, I wouldn't say she's strict," she answered, trying her best to not come across as uncomfortable as she felt.

Mr. Wright nodded. June glanced back at the front door, hoping Roxie would soon return. She figured Jim was simply trying to make small talk, but the conversation was undeniably awkward. At work, she could talk to anyone about most anything, whether it be jewelry related or not. She was suddenly very aware of the fact that Mr. Wright was a near-stranger. As much as she liked him, she couldn't shake the feeling of discontentment as they sat together, just the two of them.

It was then she recalled their initial meeting at Randolphs. His demeanor had changed so dramatically at the sight of Lorraine. Since then, June had essentially written off their odd first encounter – but, *why is he asking about her now?*

The boisterous voice of Mrs. Wright then filled the room as she opened the front door.

"Sorry about that! It was a bit of a trek out there – he's workin' on the yard now," she said, grabbing her drink from the table. "Are you ready to swim, dear?"

The Wrights' swimming pool included both a diving board and slide. There was a covered area off to the side, lined with cushioned chaise lounges. Some sort of outdoor storage cabinet located behind the chairs contained rows of neatly stacked beach towels. Large hedges offered both privacy and separation from the rest of the massive backyard.

Roxie made herself comfortable in one of the chaise lounges, scrolling through her phone and sipping a drink. Jim had excused himself once she and Mrs. Wright made their way out back. Though she felt certain she was merely overthinking their exchange over brunch, she was relieved to learn that he wouldn't be joining in on their pool day.

The cool water was a welcome relief from the heat. She reveled in having the entire pool to herself, swimming from one end to the other. She couldn't help but feel some remorse for leaving her father to run the shop on his own for the day. She didn't mind working, in fact, she enjoyed it most days. Though, she couldn't escape the fact that she had long held some sort of resentment for not having the free time that most of her classmates enjoyed.

The day passed quickly, with the pair moving back indoors after about an hour in the summer sun. The Wrights' family room included a large, flat screen TV, which featured virtually every streaming service known to man. They also owned about a dozen large binders, which contained hundreds of DVD's, organized alphabetically.

They weren't ten minutes into the film *Polyanna* before Mrs. Wright headed to the kitchen to fix a plate of leftovers for the two of them. June couldn't remember the last time she'd felt so relaxed.

"You know, June, you're welcome anytime you like. It's not easy for me to admit, but I've missed having company since we moved here," she said as she returned from clearing their plates.

"I'd love to come back another day," she replied, realizing she was secretly hoping Mrs. Wright would extend an invitation.

"I'm glad, dear," Roxie said, smiling. "You see, Jim has been pretty preoccupied lately – new house and all."

She nodded. June had to admit to herself that she enjoyed being doted on for a change. But it was more than that – spending time with Roxie was effortless. They didn't need a mediator to communicate. They could even sit in comfortable silence for an extended period of time, with no rush to fill the void.

"I'll be here as much as you like, Mrs. Wright."

CHAPTER NINE

Several weeks had passed since June's first visit to the home of Mr. and Mrs. Wright. She had grown accustomed to spending a lot of time there – laying out by the pool and binge-watching TV. Roxie kept the fridge fully stocked; and as June was often reminded, she was welcome to anything. The pair enjoyed taking walks around the property when cloud coverage offered some relief from the heat. It was on these walks that she learned more about the Wrights' life prior to Jim's retirement.

Mr. Wright had developed a computer software which resulted in the subsequent launch of his company while in his late-thirties. Though she never held an official job title, Roxie served as his personal assistant until he decided to sell the business and retire. June was impressed by the fact that the Wrights had spent so much time together throughout their marriage, yet still seemed to enjoy one another's company.

Though her father would never admit it, she knew that her spending so much time away from the shop was causing a strain on him. Despite Lorraine frequently expressing her disapproval, her father would always insist that he was happy she was enjoying her summer break. While she hated that he was having to work harder than usual, she reasoned that he could easily hire someone else if the workload became too much. *Maybe we should have hired some help a long time ago –*

it's really not fair that I've had to work every summer, she thought as she and Roxie made their way out the front door of the Wright home.

The day was perfect for staying outdoors – overcast and not too hot. The hydrangeas blew gently in the wind as the pair admired the massive garden. Luca had spent most of the morning pulling weeds and adding mulch where needed.

Though she wasn't accustomed to having a lot in common with boys her age, she found that Luca was very easy to talk to. With his mother being an 'English Lit' teacher (as he called it), he was well-versed on the subject. Roxie would frequently invite him inside for snacks, which often lead to in depth discussions of classic works such as *The Scarlet Letter* and *Lord of the Flies*.

Jim never partook in any such dialogue. Though he was always friendly, he seemed to spend much of his time either at the hardware store or pacing the property, looking for projects for Luca. It was apparent to June that Mr. Wright was not a 'handy' person. Though he was constantly overseeing Luca's work, he just didn't seem the type to get his hands dirty. Even a task as elementary as tightening a handle on a kitchen cabinet was outsourced to Luca. It seemed as if nothing could get past him – from a creaky door to the slightest of separation in crown molding.

"How's it going, Luca?" Roxie asked, as she and June made their way over to him.

"I may need a few more bags of mulch… but I think it's lookin' good," he replied.

"Oh, yes – beautiful! How would you feel about repainting the shutters this week – I'm just not quite sold on the color."

"No problem. Would you like me to grab some paint swatches from Hasting's before I head over tomorrow?" he asked.

"Thank you, dear. I think we'll stay in the gray-family, just may need to go a bit darker."

"Sounds good," he said as he gathered empty bags of mulch from the ground. "Well, I think I'll call it a day. I'll see you ladies in the morning. I mean... June, you plan on being here tomorrow?"

"Oh, yes... I mean, I plan on it," she replied.

It seemed to her as if the world outside the Wrights' front gate was slowly fading away. She didn't care to expend any mental energy trying to figure out what her mother might be hiding – in fact, she'd grown increasingly indifferent toward her over the past few weeks. Similarly, Ethan Morris and his friends were of no concern to her – she felt as if a million miles away from it all.

"Let's go on in the house, sweetie. I bet Jim's got something whipped up for lunch if you'd like to stay," Mrs. Wright said as they waved goodbye to Luca.

As she and Roxie settled in at the kitchen table, Mr. Wright served ham and cheese sliders. They were topped with some sort of poppy seed glaze, and paired nicely with pasta salad on the side. Jim had a knack for cooking. He was particularly skillful when it came to using his grill, which sat on the back patio of the home.

There was also an outdoor sink and small refrigerator. Roxie, on the other hand, rarely utilized their gourmet-style kitchen. She did, however, seem to enjoy making frequent trips to the grocery store and "supporting local eateries," as she put it.

"Well, Miss. June – did you get a good look at the hydrangeas? That Luca's doing a fine job with the yard," Jim inquired as he refilled his wife's glass of tea.

"I did… they're beautiful," she replied. "I've always wished we could have a garden – of course there's nothing but concrete around Randolphs."

"Oh yeah, that *is* a shame. Maybe you ladies should get you one of those window boxes for your birthday. That way you could plant some flowers for yourself at home."

"I'd never thought of that. Wow, you have a great memory, Mr. Wright – I don't even remember mentioning my birthday is coming up."

"Oh yeah, well… you must of said it in passing," he said, stumbling over his words a bit.

"Well there's an idea," Roxie interjected. "Of course, you should take some time and think about what you'd like for your special day – it can be anything, really!"

"Roxie, you've already done so much for me. I don't need anything." While grateful for the offer, she couldn't help but feel uncomfortable at the idea of the Wrights buying her any more than they already had.

"Nonsense! It's not every day a girl turns… you'll be eighteen, right?" she asked, pausing for a response.

"Yes, eighteen this Friday."

When faced with the dilemma of either registering their daughter for kindergarten once she completed preschool or holding her back for a year, Edward and Lorraine had opted for the latter. With her birthday falling in early-July, they thought it preferable for her to be one of the oldest children in her class, rather than the youngest. As a result, she would be one of the first in her senior class to turn eighteen.

"Well, it's a big birthday, darling," Roxie said as she served herself more pasta salad. "How'd you like to make a trip to Mathilde's Salon?"

At the suggestion, June couldn't help but smile. The next day, June sat waiting next to Mrs. Wright. The hairdresser with whom they'd booked an appointment was finishing up with another customer. They watched as she styled the hair of a woman in her late-thirties, sporting what looked to be a fresh cut and highlights.

All attempts to dissuade Roxie from treating her to a day at the salon proved fruitless. Though she ultimately agreed, she was shocked to learn that Mrs. Wright had somehow procured a spot for the following morning. As she'd heard her mother mention multiple times – openings at Mathilde's Salon were typically difficult to come by.

She had spent most of her evening scrolling through Pinterest in search of inspiration for a new haircut. Though her hair was undeniably beautiful, it sorely lacked in any sort of styling – falling like heavy drapes around her face. While her mother had made a few attempts throughout the years to persuade her to do more with it than just her usual trim, she'd never had any real interest in changing up her look. Her hair was thick – making styling it herself a bit time-consuming. As a result, she had always opted for keeping it as low-maintenance as possible.

"Do you know what you'd like to have done, dear?" Mrs. Wright inquired.

She had narrowed it down to two options, both of which were saved as screenshots on her phone. As she showed Roxie the photos of two different women, each donning vastly different cuts, it occurred to her that her mother might not appreciate her changing her hair without so much as a heads-up beforehand.

While her father remained unwavering in his support of her newfound freedom, Lorraine was less enthused with how her daughter was spending her summer break. Though for the past week or two, she'd seemed to have reached at least some sort of acceptance regarding June's friendship with Mrs. Wright. At least, she'd ceased protesting – which June assumed was at the behest of her father.

"Well, I think either one of those would look wonderful on you, sweetie," Roxie said as she handed the phone back.

"This one would just be taking off an inch or two… and maybe some long layers to give it more of a style," June said as she ran her fingers through her long, brown hair. "And this one… of course, it would be a pretty big change," she said, staring at the photo in front of her.

"Of course, it's completely up to you… but if you don't mind me saying so, dear – I happen to think change is good for a person every now and again," Mrs. Wright said, waving at the saleswoman who'd helped them on their previous shopping trip at the boutique.

At this, June glanced at herself in a nearby mirror. She wore a patterned skirt, paired with a stark white top which donned large ruffles at the sleeves.

"Though, I'd take my advice with a grain of salt… I'm a bit of a risk taker myself," Roxie continued, gesturing towards her own outfit, which included her usual six-inch heels and flamboyant color combinations.

"Well, you always make it work," June retorted with a grin.

Minutes later she sat nervously as the hairdresser draped a black cape around her shoulders. Mrs. Wright had made her way over to the boutique, promising to return once she'd procured a 'decent summer blouse' for herself. June took one final look at her phone before deleting one of the photos.

"So! What are we doing today?" the hairdresser asked, smiling as she began to comb through her long locks.

"Let's chop it off," she replied, showing her the photo. She had finally decided that the image of a woman modeling a 'bob' haircut would be the inspiration for her new look.

It was nearly lunchtime before the pair made their way to the front of Mathilde's to pay for both the salon appointment, as well as Roxie's new haul of clothes from the boutique. Mrs. Wright had not stopped gushing over her young friend's new haircut, which lay gracefully just above her collarbone. As she had never before mustered up the courage to cut more than a few inches of her hair at a time, June hardly recognized herself as she gazed at the full-length mirror closest to the changing room.

"Oh, I meant to book an appointment with the salon for myself, dear. Would you mind taking care of this? It's the pink card in my wallet," Mrs. Wright said, handing over her purse.

An employee began to ring them up as June placed each item of clothing onto the counter. Though she'd been horrendously uncomfortable with the idea of Mrs. Wright paying for her clothes only weeks prior, she had grown to a certain level of comfort over time. Somehow, rifling through her purse didn't seem all that peculiar.

She was surprised to find the wallet a bit unorganized – crammed full of cards and crumpled receipts. As she handed over Mrs. Wright's credit card, several pieces of paper fell onto the floor in a heap. June couldn't help but take notice of an old photograph, which had landed face up in front of the counter.

The photo was that of a newborn baby girl. She wore a white, smocked dress and matching bonnet. The photo was a bit tattered around the edges, though she could clearly see the face of the child looking back at her. Her dress and hat both appeared a bit oversized for the tiny baby.

It was then that she noticed Mrs. Wright as she made her way toward the checkout counter. She hurriedly gathered everything from the floor and began to stuff receipts back into the wallet.

"I'm sorry, June – I should have warned you my wallet was such a disaster!" Roxie exclaimed; her arm outstretched to help her up from the floor.

She felt a sudden pain in the pit of her stomach as she handed the old photograph to Mrs. Wright, who remained uncharacteristically silent as she took a few moments to stare at the image in front of her. *I hope she doesn't think I was snooping,* June thought, a bit panicked.

She noticed her friend looking slightly flushed as she signed her receipt and thanked the woman at checkout. The pair then made their way outside with bags in tow, into the heat of the summer sun.

She couldn't help but feel that she had inadvertently invaded Mrs. Wright's privacy. Even the high of a new look wasn't enough to negate her racing thoughts on the drive back to the Wright home. She couldn't help but breathe a sigh of relief as Roxie finally broke the silence.

"I'm sorry if I haven't been myself since we left Mathilde's… I don't want you to think you did anything wrong, Bug." June remained silent as Mrs. Wright took a drink of water before continuing. "The picture I keep in my wallet… it, brings up a lot of emotions for me. I honestly forget it's there with all the junk I've been meaning to clean out."

As they pulled into the driveway, Mrs. Wright parked several yards shy of her usual spot near the house. June noticed that Luca was working in the flowerbeds again. She watched as the wind blew an empty bag of mulch from the bed of his truck.

"You see, dear – Jim and I lost a baby when we were very young. In fact, we were just in high school at the time," she said, clearly holding back tears. "She was born with a heart condition… we never made it home with her." She then pulled the worn photo gingerly from her wallet. "The hospital took this the day she was born."

June sat in stunned silence as she once again looked at the tattered photograph. "I'm so sorry, Mrs. Wright," she said, desperately trying to find her words. "She's beautiful."

"Thank you, honey," she replied, wiping tears from her eyes as she pulled a small, compact mirror from her console. "I hope you understand why you're so special to me, June… I never had the chance to do any of these things with my own little girl." She went on to explain that although she and Jim married sometime after graduating high school, they'd been unsuccessful in their attempts to have another child.

After taking the time to fix her makeup, Mrs. Wright continued down the long driveway, parking next to Luca's truck. Though it was a heavy topic, June could tell that their conversation had proven cathartic for Roxie, as she patted her hand before reaching for her many shopping bags.

"Sorry we weren't here earlier, Luca," Mrs. Wright said as she made her way over to him. "Did you happen to have a chance to stop by the paint store?"

"Yes ma'am, I did," he said, opening the door of his truck and retrieving a bag of paint swatches from the passenger seat.

June couldn't help but notice his look of surprise as she greeted him.

"Wow, you cut your hair... I mean, it looks very nice," he said, offering her a reassuring smile.

"It was just... time for a change," she said as she ran her fingers through her freshly styled locks. She was still getting used to how light she felt after cutting off nearly a foot of hair.

"I just can't get over how precious it looks on her," Mrs. Wright interjected.

Luca grinned as she moved on to the topic of paint color.

"Well, I think I know what I'd like to go with, but I suppose I'll run it by Jim just to be sure," she said, pointing to a warm-gray color on one of the swatches. "I'll let you know by Thursday for sure."

"Sure thing; I'll be here," he replied, loading his things into the bed of his truck. "I really like your hair, June. It suits you," he said, as she somehow managed to contain her smile.

Though she had never invested much in her appearance, priding herself on being 'low-maintenance,' she couldn't help but feel a sense of elation as she tousled her hair in the Wrights' downstairs bathroom, as Roxie warmed up leftovers for lunch. It wasn't just the new clothes and shorter hairstyle – she felt a sense of confidence like she'd never experienced.

She wondered why it had taken her so long to get to this point. Perhaps she had stiff-armed anything which her mother deemed important out of sheer pride. She never wanted to be like her mother, nor did she care to conform to a standard set by her peers.

Though as she stood staring at her reflection, she couldn't help but wish Ethan Morris and his friends could see her now.

CHAPTER TEN

"Let's go ahead and close up, Bug. Wouldn't anyone in their right mind get out in this mess," Edward said as he locked the front door of the shop. "Any updates?"

"Not really... the severe storm warning is still in effect for three more hours," June said, scrolling through her weather app.

"Well, I hate it couldn't have been a nicer day for your birthday."

"Oh, I don't care about that – it's just another day," she responded, never taking her eyes off the phone.

"Come on now, Bug. At least with the storm we can start our celebrations off early," he said optimistically. "You know you like that cake your mama picked up from the bakery."

Though neither acknowledged it, she knew that the dynamic between herself and her father was a bit off. Her parents had been predictably taken aback by her drastic change in hairstyle a few days prior. She had never in her life spent so much time away from home, nor had she made any big decisions without discussing it with them beforehand. Though as the initial shock wore off, both seemed to approve of her new cut.

While the resentment she felt remained unwavering, June did notice that her mother was making more of an effort with her than she had in a long time, despite the fact that she was clearly still uncomfortable with her friendship with Mrs. Wright. For the past several days, Lorraine had taken the time to ask about her day over dinner, though June offered nothing more than brief, generic responses.

It had taken a fair amount of begging on her father's part to procure assurance that she would spend her birthday at home. While she did feel a certain amount of remorse for her absence the past few weeks, she couldn't help but wish she were spending the day at the Wright home.

However, she did have to admit she was looking forward to dessert. Despite the storm, Lorraine had picked up June's favorite cake earlier in the day — coconut with cream cheese frosting. She had also stopped for one of her favorite 'take and bake' casseroles from a local bistro for dinner.

As the pair made their way inside their second-floor apartment, she noticed several nicely wrapped gifts sitting on the kitchen counter. Her mother was busy stirring a pitcher of sweet tea as she hummed an indistinguishable tune. Edward took the time to compliment his wife on the cleanliness of the apartment, with June taking the opportunity to head back toward her bedroom.

"Wait, Bug! Why don't you stay in here with us? I'm sure your mama'd like to catch up," her father said as he took a seat at the kitchen table.

Reluctantly, she made her way back into the kitchen.

"You're looking tan, June," her mother commented as she took a seat at the table.

"I've been spending a lot of time outside lately. I've burned a bit on my shoulders, but Mrs. Wright is always reminding me to wear sunscreen." She noticed her mother wince at the mention of her name.

"Well, you look nice with a little color on your face," her mother said as she poured herself a glass of tea.

June wondered how she managed to make even a compliment come across as snarky.

"I *like* being outdoors… it's a nice change," June quickly retorted, staring out the window as a lightning bolt lit up the sky.

"Oh, come on now, Bug… what about the watermelon festival? That's always been a good chance for us to stretch our legs," her father interjected. "In fact, how'd you ladies like to go this year – saw online it's gonna be next weekend."

"I've missed our little bed and breakfast," Lorraine answered him, smiling. "I think that'd be nice. What about you, June?"

"Uh, maybe. We'll see. It's kind of a long drive just for watermelons."

The prospect of being stuck in a car with her mother was a situation she wished to avoid at all costs. At this, neither Edward nor Lorraine responded.

"So, what time you ladies think you'd like to eat?" her father asked, breaking the silence.

Though her mother was unusually talkative at dinner, June found it difficult to participate in the conversation. Edward suggested they play a few rounds of Rummikub following cake and coffee. The game was a family favorite, and she couldn't help but enjoy herself as they sat around their kitchen table, engaged in competitive play.

For a moment, June forgot about all that had transpired over the past several weeks. She wasn't thinking about her mother's secretive phone conversation, nor her discovery that she was in contact with a private investigator as she excitedly announced her victory upon tallying up final scores.

"Alright, Bug – how 'bout you open up your gifts," her father said, rising from his chair.

She didn't know what to expect – she hadn't asked for anything. June did have to concede that despite her shortcomings, her mother was an exceptional gift giver. Lorraine enjoyed shopping, and she was good at it. Her gifts were always well thought out, and she spared no expense.

Opening the first package, she could sense her father's excitement. Inside she found a dainty, white gold locket. A delicate floral pattern engraved along the edges perfectly accented the piece. Inscribed in the center of the locket were the words 'June Bug,' written in cursive lettering. She couldn't help but smile as she opened it.

"We didn't put any pictures in it yet… wanted to let you pick them out," Edward said, grinning back at his wife. "Your mama helped me out with the design — I think it turned out real well."

"I love it. Thank you, guys," she said, draping the chain around her neck.

The next box she opened contained a pale, buttery-yellow cardigan. She immediately recognized the gift box and tissue paper as coming from Mathilde's. It looked like something June would have chosen for herself.

"Alright, one more," Lorraine said, smiling warmly. "Just be careful opening it."

She noticed the sheen of white glass as she pulled back sheets of tissue paper which were surrounding the piece. It was a Fenton vase. She recognized the design as being 'hobnail,' which consists of protruding knob-like bumps along the surface of the glass.

She recalled mentioning to her mother a while back how much she liked the milk glass pieces she'd collected over the years, though she found it hard to believe that she would remember. Turning the piece over in her hand, she took a moment to admire the beauty of the glass.

"It's from the mid-50's," her mother said excitedly. "If you like, we could keep it in the curio cabinet… or we could find somewhere in your room. It's up to you."

June encountered a flood of different emotions as she gazed upon the vase she held in her hands. It was a kind gesture on her mother's part. She knew that she was extending a proverbial 'olive branch,' and desperately wished she could receive it as such. She couldn't help but feel, however, that the time for such a gesture had long since passed. She knew that the resentment and anger she felt couldn't be swept under the rug in one night, with one beautiful vase.

"Thanks, Mom. It's great," she said, setting it gingerly on the countertop.

While she couldn't fault Lorraine for trying, it just wasn't enough. She doubted that the underlying friction between herself and her mother would ever go away.

The next morning, June lay still as she listened to the sound of rain pounding against her bedroom window. The storm had continued throughout the night, with no signs of letting up. She watched as the numbers on her old alarm clock blinked, as they had lost power several times during the night.

She hoped they wouldn't be opening the shop for the day, or at least until the storm let up a bit. She reached around for her phone, which she thought must be buried somewhere within her covers. She'd stayed up late scrolling through social media, in an attempt to track down any new developments in the Ethan Morris-saga.

It seemed to her that things had more or less died down since the incident, as the online chatter had subsided. Apart from her absence, it was business as usual at Randolphs. According to her father, sales were right on track with the previous summer, despite the fact that he was carrying most of the load.

It seemed the majority of her class had returned from their summer vacations, including Reagan, who had made several attempts to meet up with June. She wasn't sure why she kept putting her off, other than the fact that she enjoyed spending every moment she could at the Wright home. She relished spending her days by the pool – having long talks with Roxie, who always seemed to be fully present, giving her undivided attention.

The aroma of cinnamon rolls filled the air as she made her way into the kitchen. She was surprised to find her parents eating breakfast together, already dressed for the day.

"Mornin,' Bug, how'd the storm treat ya last night? Sleep okay?" her father asked.

"I slept fine – it was kind of peaceful, actually."

"Yeah, I'm with you there," he said, fetching himself another roll. "You're not dressed yet?"

"Well, I didn't know if we'd be opening this morning... it's still pretty crazy out there," she said, glancing at the window.

"Oh, I don't think it's quite as bad as it's been, and the news says we should be in the clear before this afternoon."

She hoped her disappointment wasn't too apparent as she grabbed a cinnamon roll for herself.

"Well, I'm sure it'll be really slow… if we have anyone come in at all," she said as she took a seat next to her father. Lorraine stayed quiet as she flipped through a magazine.

"Customers have pieces they needed to pick up this weekend… want to make sure we're here for 'em."

"That's true," she replied, knowing his mind was made up. "So… what would you think if I went over to the Wrights for a while?" she asked cautiously.

At this, Lorraine looked up from her magazine. "June, you've been spending a lot of time over there. Your dad could really use your help today," she said, looking over at her husband.

Why does she care? June wondered as she studied her father's face, looking for a reaction. "It's going to be slow today. I really don't need to be here," she said defiantly.

"Yes, you do," her mother responded, never breaking eye contact. "In fact, your father and I have been meaning to talk to you about how you've been spending your time lately."

"With the Wrights?" she asked, though she had no doubt as to the answer.

"Yes. I'm not sure it's appropriate for you to be spending so much time over there. Why don't you see some of your friends for a change?"

"I like being there. Mrs. Wright is my friend… she listens to me." June could feel the anger she'd held back for so long rising up inside of her. She knew that her mother didn't care for Mrs. Wright, but it didn't matter.

"We listen to you too, June. You know your father and I love you," her mother said, her lower lip quivering slightly.

"Maybe Dad does."

"Excuse me? What are you saying?" Lorraine asked, the hurt she clearly felt written all over her face.

"You don't need to lie anymore, Mom. I know how you feel about me," she replied, rising from the table as her father looked on in stunned silence.

"Honestly, June, what are you talking about? You are my daughter – of course I love you! I wouldn't lie to you," she said, standing to meet her at eye level.

"Really? So why are you talking to a private investigator?" Her whole body now shook uncontrollably.

Lorraine's eyes grew larger as she stood staring at her daughter, seemingly unable to speak. At this, Edward placed his hand on the small of his wife's back in support.

"Woah now, what are you talking about? Your mama isn't talking to an investigator," he said, his voice raised slightly.

"I guess I'm not the only one you're dishonest with," she said, looking at her mother, who was clearly in shock at the sudden turn of events. "That's it. I'm going to my room," she said, starting down the hallway despite her father's demands to stay put.

Locking the door behind her, she listened intently as her father started questioning Lorraine, a hint of anger in his voice. Though she tried desperately to keep her emotions in check, the tears began to flow as she gave up on eavesdropping in on her parents' conversation.

Her thoughts raced as she buried her face in her still-shaking hands. She had never planned on calling her out the way she did – it just happened. Whatever the repercussions might be, she wasn't going to wait around to face them.

She knew she had to get out of that apartment. It wouldn't be long before either one of them would be knocking at her door, demanding an appearance. She headed quickly to her closet where she hastily changed into a pair of jeans and summer blouse. Hitting her knees, she searched for her Converse sneakers, which she hadn't worn in weeks.

June quickly stuffed her phone and keys into her crossbody purse. She then took a moment to take a deep breath while pulling her hair back into a ponytail and through a baseball cap. Shaking, she wiped the lenses of her eyeglasses with a cloth, which had grown foggy due to the tears streaming down her face.

There was a large tree just outside her bedroom window. She had used it several times before over the years to make her way down to the street without her parents' knowledge. However, it had always been something she'd done merely for a thrill. She had never sought to actually *leave* undetected. She had also never climbed it during a massive downpour.

She knew she couldn't just go waltzing out the front door after a confrontation like that. Though her mind was made up, she shuddered a bit as she carefully opened her second-story window. Rain poured inside as she made her way onto the steep roof. Grabbing ahold of a large tree limb with one arm, she managed to close her bedroom window with the other. The limb shook as she hoisted her body on top of it and began to crawl slowly towards the trunk of the tree. Though she tried desperately to steady her knees, her efforts proved fruitless as she inched further from her bedroom window.

By the time she made it to the base of the tree her slender frame was soaked through. She took a moment to once again wipe down her fogged glasses. She adjusted her ball cap before taking the short jump from the bottom limb onto the grass below. As she quickly made her way to the small parking lot located directly behind Randolphs, she glanced back at her bedroom window.

Though relieved to make it safely to her car and out of the storm, the tears once again began to flow as she laid her head on the steering wheel. She didn't know where she would go. She hadn't thought it through before escaping the apartment. She wondered if the Wrights would simply call her parents should she show up on their doorstep, unannounced and soaking wet. She could see Mrs. Wright not wanting them to worry.

After taking a few minutes to compose herself, she decided for the time being to head to Hank's, one of the only restaurants in town that included a drive-through window. Although they wouldn't open for a few hours, she reasoned that waiting out the storm in their parking lot made more sense than staying put. She didn't want to risk her parents checking to see if her car was still at the apartment.

There wasn't another vehicle in sight as she made it to Hank's. The storm raged on as she pulled into a secluded spot behind the building. Pulling her knees to her chest, she grabbed her phone before reclining her seat and laying back against the headrest. Rather than think about all that had transpired earlier in the day, she decided it best to scroll mindlessly through social media, in an attempt to block it all out. She was emotionally exhausted – her thoughts cloudy and irrational. She needed to rest. She needed the thoughts to subside, if only for a little while.

Sometime later, June felt her body jerk as a loud noise suddenly startled her from her sleep. Looking out the passenger-side window she could see that an employee of Hank's was throwing trash bags into their dumpster, located mere feet from where she was parked. It wasn't until she saw the clock that she realized she'd fallen asleep. The lunch crowd filled the parking lot, as the storm had subsided to nothing more than a light shower. She watched for several minutes as raindrops hit her windshield.

Though she had planned on grabbing lunch from the drive-through window, she found herself wanting to get out and stretch her legs after her accidental nap in the driver's seat. She pulled down her mirror, staring at her reflection as she attempted to smooth her thick hair. It had halfway dried while still under her baseball cap. *No one will notice me anyway*, she thought as she made her way out of the car.

The dining room was relatively busy. She figured people were anxious to get out after the storm had let up. She couldn't help but shiver a bit as she placed her order at the front counter. Her clothing hadn't dried much since her time spent scaling a tree in the thick of the storm.

She filled her drink cup before walking toward a booth which sported dark red, leather cushioning. She had barely situated herself before hearing the voice of Ethan Morris. He had called her name in a way that seemed to her as being less-than-friendly. Though, admittedly, she was already on edge. She didn't wish to speak to anyone, let alone *him*.

"Miss. Randolph, fancy seeing you here. What'd you do, take a dip in a pond?" he said as his friends snickered behind him.

"I'm really not in the mood to talk right now, Ethan," she said, directing her attention back to the tray of food in front of her.

"Oh, come on, now. I didn't mean it like that. In fact, I've been hoping I might run into you," he said, never breaking eye contact as she once again looked up at him. "I've been meaning to apologize to both you and your dad."

She couldn't tell whether he was being sincere, but it really didn't matter. She didn't have the mental energy to deal with him; it was all just too much for one day. *He needs to leave me alone.*

"Okay, that's fine, Ethan," she said, taking a sip of her drink. She hoped her body language would be enough for him to get the message that she wanted him to leave.

"No, really. I *am* sorry. It was a stupid thing to do," he said, staring intently. "We never should have tried to pull something like that. It wasn't funny."

"I SAID it's fine!" she yelled; her eyes locked in on his.

He stood motionless as his friends looked on in silence. Though clearly shaken by her reaction, Ethan managed a small nod of his head before heading back to his table. While she found it hard to believe that she could hurt the feelings of someone like Ethan, she couldn't help but feel a twinge of guilt as she quickly finished her burger and headed out the front door of the restaurant.

Her cheeks once again filled with warm tears as she made it back to her car. She had an overwhelming feeling of dread as her breathing grew heavy and labored. Starting the car, she blasted cool air onto her face as she grew increasingly dizzy and weak. She struggled to catch her breath, trying in vain to stop crying.

It took nearly twenty minutes before she felt ready to leave the parking lot. She hated feeling so out of control. It seemed as though everything was falling apart.

She knew that her parents had yet to discover her absence, as she didn't have any missed calls – though it was just a matter of time. *I bet they've at least knocked on my door... it's locked. They must think I'm sleeping – or just ignoring them.* As she pulled back onto the street, she knew where she was going, even if she hadn't yet acknowledged it to herself. *Mrs. Wright won't call them — I know she won't.*

CHAPTER ELEVEN

As she drove to the home of Jim and Roxanne, she wondered how her relationship with not only her mother, but also her father, had deteriorated so quickly. It felt as if her family life would never be the same after such a confrontation. She and her parents had always tended to sweep things under the proverbial rug in the past, and she didn't know how they might react upon her return.

She anticipated a call or text at any moment. Glancing down at her phone which sat upright in one of her cupholders, she wondered what her father must be dealing with. Having just learned of his wife's deception – *he must be so confused. Could they still be arguing?* She knew her mother wouldn't be able to explain it all away this time. She would have to come clean. *Won't she? She's been lying to him. Who knows what else she's lied about?*

As she pulled up to the home where she had spent so much time the past several weeks, she felt an undeniable sense of relief. Spotting Mrs. Wright as she arranged potted plants by the front door, she made one last attempt to gather her composure before exiting the car. She didn't want to alarm anyone, especially not Roxie. She just needed to be *somewhere* she felt safe. She needed *someone* whom she could trust. She never wanted to feel as though a burden, but she desperately needed a friend.

"What a surprise, dear. I wasn't expecting to see you today!" Roxie exclaimed, grinning from ear to ear as she made her way down the driveway. Though she never intended to trouble her with all that had transpired earlier in the day, June found herself unable to mask her anguish. Without hesitation, Mrs. Wright wrapped her arms around her young friend as tears once again flowed freely down her face.

The pair made their way inside the house, settling on the living room couch before June felt ready to speak. Mrs. Wright listened intently as she shared details of the confrontation which had led to her sneaking out. She held nothing back, and Roxie remained silent as she spoke.

Though she felt certain there was nothing Mrs. Wright could say to make her feel better about the situation, it was a relief just to be able to talk it through with someone — someone who cared.

"Can I get you something to drink?" Mrs. Wright asked, looking concerned. "You don't look well, sweetie."

Though she had yet to respond, Roxie made her way toward the kitchen. In her absence, she once again buried her face in her now shaking hands. *Will they even want me to come home? Why did I do that? I bet Mom hates me even more now.* Her breathing grew increasingly labored. She laid her hand at her chest as she could feel that her heart was now pounding rapidly. She tried in vain to catch her breath. It was as if the spell she'd had while still parked at Hank's was once again rushing over her body like a wave.

Mrs. Wright returned with a glass of ice water in tow. June tried desperately to focus on something other than her current state of mind. She could hear Roxie hurriedly making her way over to her, hastily placing the glass on a nearby coffee table. Though she wrapped her arms around her, June felt as alone as ever. It felt as if *nothing* would ever be okay again.

Roxie began stroking her hair as June tried once again to slow her breathing. She felt as if she was dying, right there on the Wrights' sofa. She knew it was irrational, yet couldn't escape the racing thoughts.

"We'll get through this, darling," Roxie said, continuing to gently stroke her hair. "I get them too. It will pass. I promise."

Sometime later, June lifted her head slowly from the pillow which Roxie had given her following what she knew to be a panic attack. She hadn't intended on falling asleep, but the physical and emotional toll of the day had left her exhausted. At the behest of Mrs. Wright, she had made herself comfortable on their living room couch, which felt more like an expensive mattress.

She felt her stomach turn as she tried in vain to locate her cell phone. *How long have I been asleep!? I bet they've called a hundred times by now!* Mrs. Wright was nowhere to be found as she lifted the soft, white blanket that was draped over her body. Unable to find her phone, she walked quickly to the kitchen. The oven clock confirmed her fears, as she realized it had been nearly three hours since her arrival.

She called out for Mrs. Wright as she headed back to the living room and hurriedly slipped on her shoes which lay next to the couch. Her anxiety increased as she lifted each and every throw pillow in search of her phone. *Did I leave it in the car? Dad must be so worried!*

She had just reached the front door when she heard Roxie call her name from the top of the stairs.

"June, sweetie. How do you feel? I'm so glad you were able to rest a bit."

"I... I'm fine. I just... do you remember if I brought my phone inside?" She placed her hand to her head as she spoke. She knew it was likely stress causing her to feel a bit disoriented.

June noticed that Jim had now emerged from one of the second-story bedrooms.

"You feelin' okay? You're lookin' a bit pale, June," he said as he made his way down the steps, followed closely by his wife.

"I'm okay... I think I just stood up too quickly," she said as Roxie put her arm around her.

"Why don't we just get you to the guest room so you can rest a bit more. I know you must be exhausted," Mrs. Wright said as she led her to the foot of the stairs.

"Oh... no, thank you. I really need to find my phone. My parents must know I'm gone by now. I need to let them know I'm okay," she said, trying to mask the panic in her voice.

"I really must insist you come upstairs, Bug. We'll get everything sorted out – I promise," Mrs. Wright said, placing her hand on the small of June's back.

She didn't know what was happening as she conceded to heading up the stairs. Something in Roxie's voice had changed. Her tone was still pleasant. Her words were still kind… but something was *off*.

Mrs. Wright patted her back as they made it to the second floor, leading her down the hallway. Jim stopped in front of them as he reached the final door at the end of the hall – the pink bedroom.

"Why don't we just make ourselves comfortable in here," Mrs. Wright said. "I know how much you love this room."

Though their behavior was undeniably odd, she remained relatively unworried as Roxie gestured for her to take a seat on the oversized pink bed. She wondered if they were merely concerned due to her panicked state upon her arrival earlier in the day.

"I'm really okay now," she blurted out, as Roxie took a seat next to her. "I know why you're worried… but I'm really fine." Though in reality she was far from being 'okay,' June was determined to say whatever it took to convince the Wrights otherwise.

"No, sweetheart. You're not," Mrs. Wright said as she motioned for Jim to take a seat on the velvet-covered bench at the foot of the bed. "I don't think your family situation is healthy for you," she continued. "And I'm not just saying that because of what happened today… Jim and I have been concerned for a while now."

She knew she shouldn't have broken down in front of Mrs. Wright the way she did. It was bound to upset her, as she was such a compassionate person.

"No, no, I'm sorry… this is all my fault," June said as she began nervously running her fingers through the ends of her hair. "Everything is fine at home. My mom and I have just hit a bit of a rough patch lately," she reiterated, desperately trying to reassure them.

She noticed as the Wrights exchanged a quick glance between them, yet said nothing. Roxie then walked slowly to the bedroom window, as if to think.

"How do you like this room, dear?" she asked.

"I… the room? It's beautiful, Roxie," she responded, clearly confused by the seemingly sudden change in topic.

"It can be yours, my dear. You can stay with us… as long as you like," she said, once again gazing out the second-story window.

June found herself struggling to process her thoughts – it was all just too much. She knew she had to fix it but wasn't sure how. She had never really allowed herself to confide in anyone concerning the difficulties between herself and her mother. Now that she had, it felt as though a huge mistake.

"I'm so sorry, Roxie, if I gave you the wrong impression about my family. I promise you everything is fine at home, it's just… normal mother-daughter stuff."

Jim sat quietly as his wife made her way over to him at the foot of the bed. Placing her hands on his shoulders, she stared longingly at the large painting that hung just above the ornate headboard.

"Do you see that little girl?" Roxie asked.

She nodded. "Yes, ma'am."

"I come in here almost every day just to look at that painting... just to see that little girl," she continued, her voice beginning to crack. "And she's not even real, June. She doesn't exist."

"Where did she come from, Mrs. Wright?" she asked tentatively.

"Jim and I had this commissioned soon after our wedding day. She's what we imagined our little girl would have looked like at that age," she responded as Jim handed her a handkerchief from his shirt pocket. "She would have been nearly three years old when we married."

June looked once again at the painting hung so gracefully in its antique-gold frame. The child staring back at her did, indeed, look to be about three years old. Her hair curled at the ends, particularly around the ears. The string of pearls around her neck added an air of sophistication and elegance to the otherwise-youthful piece of artwork. Her style of dress looked to be from the late-1800s, rather than what would have been appropriate for a child in the early 1980s (the time in which June assumed the Wrights would have married).

"Jim and I didn't have much for the artist to go on. We showed him our one photograph of her as a newborn, but that was it," Mrs. Wright said, tears now soaking the embroidered handkerchief.

"I *am* sorry… I can't imagine what that must have been like for you," June replied, glancing over at Jim who was now standing silently next to his wife.

"Thank you, Bug. You have such a tender heart… and that's why it pains me so much to see you hurting the way you are." Mrs. Wright's bottom lip began to quiver slightly. "You see… I know what the love between a mother and her child should look like… and it's not what yours has been able to give you, sweetie."

"Mrs. Wright… I'm sorry, but… I really need to let my parents know that I'm okay. I need to get home now."

"I won't let her hurt you anymore, dear. She doesn't love you – not the way I do."

"Mrs. Wright, I have to go now," she said as she rose from the bed. At this, Jim moved quickly toward the bedroom door. Looking up at him, June knew she wouldn't be leaving. Her body began to shake as she stood paralyzed with fear. Her mouth suddenly felt dry, and she struggled to swallow.

"Sweetie, don't worry about a thing. We just want what's best for you. Now just come and sit back down and we'll get this all sorted out, just like I said we would."

She made her way slowly back toward Mrs. Wright, though never taking her eyes off Jim, who remained blocking the doorway. *Are they really not letting me leave? Should I scream? No one would hear me! Should I just do what they say?*

"Now I don't want you to worry about your parents making a fuss. We've taken care of that," Mrs. Wright said as June once again took a seat next to her.

"What does that mean?" she asked, her voice shaking.

"We just didn't want them to 'worry,' as you say," she responded. "While you were resting earlier, we thought it best that Jim take care of a few things."

It was then that Jim finally spoke. As he stood at the door, arms crossed, he was undeniably intimidating. He appeared somehow taller than she had ever previously noticed.

"Your folks are bound to check with us once you don't show back up after a while. I parked your car up at the bus station," he said, never once looking up at her.

Wait, what did he say? He took my car!? She felt as if the room around her was growing a bit hazy as she looked over at Mrs. Wright, who nodded her head as her husband spoke.

"Sent your father a message from your phone…" he continued, "told him you weren't coming back before I tossed it in a creek near the station," he said, his tone of voice unwavering.

"You're eighteen now, June. There's not a thing they can do about it if the police think you're just another runaway," Mrs. Wright chimed in.

Though she tried desperately to respond, the words simply didn't come. She was still in a state of shock, even entertaining the idea for a moment that she was still sleeping. *This can't be real. They wouldn't actually keep me from leaving. Mrs. Wright loves me... is Jim making her go along with this? What is happening!?*

It was then that Mrs. Wright placed her hand on June's, as if to comfort her. "We had hoped you'd come and live with us at some point after you turned eighteen, no matter what your parents had to say about it..." she continued. "After you fell asleep on the couch earlier, Jim and I discussed it – this is the perfect opportunity for you to stay here, dear... they'll think you ran away after that dreadful quarrel you all had."

This is something they've been thinking about for a while? What does she mean they discussed it? They decided to take my car and destroy my phone!?

The reality of what was happening had finally set in a bit. It was all *real*. She didn't want to even look at Mrs. Wright, but she knew she *had* to.

"But I *didn't* run away...," June said, looking up at her. "I needed space, but I was never not going back." Mrs. Wright nodded her head slightly, as if trying to seem as though sympathetic.

"I want to go home," she continued, trying to keep the conversation as friendly as she possibly could. "I've enjoyed spending time here this summer... but I don't want to live with you."

Mrs. Wright sat stone-faced for a few moments before she spoke. "I know you have an attachment to your parents, dear... but they're not good for you. I know you can't see that now, but one day you will. Trust me, I know what is best for you."

"We can provide you a life that they can't, June," Mr. Wright chimed in, still standing at the bedroom door. "We can move anywhere you want to go for your senior year... then we'll be glad to pay for college. You'll not be wanting for anything anymore."

"I just want to go home," she repeated, holding back tears. "I love my parents... again, I'm sorry if I ever gave you the wrong impression."

"Oh no, dear, we don't doubt your feelings toward them...," Mrs. Wright said as she inched closer. "I'm sorry to say, we have serious concerns about their... their attachment to *you*."

It was then that June rose suddenly to her feet. "I'd like to leave... I'd like to leave right now," she said defiantly. She didn't have a plan. There was a part of her that had still not accepted that the Wrights would legitimately stop her from leaving their home. As she made her way to the door, she could see that Mrs. Wright was now also on her feet, standing just behind her.

She tried to run. She tried desperately to make her way past Jim. She screamed, though she knew there would be no one to hear her cries. Once Mr. Wright had her arms pinned down at her sides, she tried in vain to kick him. Mrs. Wright had stepped in to assist her husband as June flailed violently, in an attempt to escape his grasp.

The struggle didn't last but a few minutes before she found herself face down on the hardwood floor, pinned by Mr. Wright, who had his knee positioned in the center of her back. He held her arms behind her as she struggled to catch her breath.

Mrs. Wright hurried out of the bedroom in search of rope, which they used to secure her to one of the four bed posts upon her return. Her knees shook violently as they tightened the ropes that held her arms tightly behind her back. Her eyes burned as the sweat and tears caused her vision to grow increasingly hazy. Her glasses had been knocked from her face at some point during the scuffle.

She still felt as though in an altered state of reality. It seemed inconceivable that Jim and Roxanne were not the people she knew them to be. She and Mrs. Wright had spent so much time together. She had trusted her completely. *How could she have fooled me?*

Though she knew it to be futile, she continued to scream as she tried in vain to free herself from the ropes which secured her to the bed post.

CHAPTER TWELVE

The next morning, June stared at the antique vanity that sat in a corner of the bedroom. Sunlight streamed in from the window, glistening as it hit the glass perfume bottles, which were arranged on silver trays atop the vanity. She didn't know how long she'd been asleep. The Wrights had decided to untie her at some point during the night. She was allowed to sleep in the bed, with the Wrights taking shifts to keep watch of her. She had completely exhausted her energy and promised she wouldn't try to run.

It was Mrs. Wright who sat in the oversized, tufted chair next to the bed as she awoke. She and Jim must have switched out at some point in the early morning hours, as she recalled watching him casually scroll through his phone just before she fell asleep. Though Roxanne looked just the same as she always had, it was as if June didn't recognize the woman sitting mere feet from her, as her eyes adjusted slowly to the morning light. This was not the woman who had befriended her mere weeks prior.

"Good morning, Bug," she said, as if nothing were amiss. "I do hope you were able to rest okay after all that unpleasantness yesterday."

She sat straight up, feeling especially vulnerable as Mrs. Wright leaned in closer. She didn't know how to respond. *Should I just act normal? Beg her to let me go?*

"I just hate that things happened the way they did. I know this is all so new and scary... but it's what is best for you, my darling."

She wanted nothing more than to scream. She wanted to lunge at her captor and fight tooth and nail until she'd made it out of that house. She hated Jim and Roxanne for what they had done to her. She hated herself in that moment for ever having trusted them.

"I think I do understand, Mrs. Wright... it's not something that I was expecting, but I know how much you care about me," she replied, trying to come across as unconfrontational as possible.

"Oh, I'm so glad to hear you say that, sweetheart," Mrs. Wright replied, looking relieved. "I never had the time I needed with my own little girl... and you, I'm sorry to say, have never had a mother to love and appreciate you the way that you deserve."

The Wrights clearly had the upper hand. They'd had time to plan everything. The measures taken thus far to conceal her whereabouts left her feeling as though an attempt to escape at this point would likely be thwarted. *Is anyone else involved? Even if I made it out the front door, I don't have the gate code.* It was then that she recalled the first time she'd met Luca – he was installing a camera outside the front door. *Does he know?*

"I suppose that's true," June responded.

Though the mere thought of keeping up a façade with Mrs. Wright made her feel sick to her stomach, she knew she needed to regain her trust.

"Could I have some water?"

"Oh my, of course dear! I know you must be starving too. Let's head downstairs as soon as you're dressed."

"But, I... I don't have any other clothes with me," she replied, looking down at her shirt, which, despite being wrinkled, had finally dried throughout the night.

"Oh yes, about that... I've taken the liberty of getting some things together for you," she said, opening the door next to the en suite bathroom. June looked on as Mrs. Wright made her way into the bedroom's massive walk-in closet. The room was packed full of clothes, shoes, and various accessories including hats, scarves, and jewelry displayed on racks that rested on a center island.

Standing from the bed, she walked slowly toward the closet, which Mrs. Wright had clearly been stocking for quite some time.

"Are these all for me?" she asked, trying desperately to mask her panic.

"Yes, they are, Bug. I'd like to think I know your taste after our little shopping trip," she said with a grin.

Once Mrs. Wright concluded her tour of both the closet and bathroom, June was allowed to shower privately while Mrs. Wright waited in the bedroom. The bathroom had also been fully-stocked – towels, toiletries, and even a variety of makeup and hair products lined the cabinets. Though she felt a sense of relief at having a moment alone, the knowledge that Mrs. Wright was lingering just outside the bathroom door left her with a sense of hopelessness. She couldn't help but sob uncontrollably as she stepped under the stream of warm water. *How long have they been planning this?*

Once she was dressed, the pair made their way downstairs where Mrs. Wright served breakfast. Though she had no appetite, she managed to nibble at a croissant, as her captor helped herself to large helpings of both bacon and smothered biscuits.

Just as Mrs. Wright had begun clearing their plates, Mr. Wright showed up.

"Oh, Jim! I'm so glad you're awake. Can I get you some juice?" his wife asked excitedly. He was clearly tired, but managed a smile and nod of his head before taking a seat next to June. Though still perplexed at how they could behave as if their morning together were just like any other day, she had reconciled to the fact that, for now, she would be following suit.

"You look refreshed, June. I'm glad to see you got yourself in some clean clothes," Jim said, glancing over at her as he reached for the pepper shaker.

"Yes, me too."

"I hope you like your new room okay… planned on setting up a little flat screen we've got stored in the closet for you," he said.

"Oh, yes! I almost forgot about that," Mrs. Wright interjected. "We have a DVD player we'll get hooked up for you too. I ordered some movies I thought you might like."

June smiled politely, though she felt certain they'd planned to bar her access to local stations, hence the DVD player. Sitting quietly as Mr. Wright finished his breakfast, she couldn't help but feel a sense of guilt as she considered what her parents must be going through. *Could they really think I ran away? How long will it take for someone to notice my car at the bus station?*

She became lost in thought as her captors continued about their morning as usual. It wasn't until she heard the familiar sound of a cell phone vibrating atop the kitchen table that she popped back into reality. It was Jim's phone. She watched as his expression turned sour, quickly making his way to the backyard. She could hear that he was speaking to someone on the other end, though the conversation lasted only seconds.

"I'll get her upstairs… you meet them outside," Mr. Wright said, slamming the door behind him.

"Already!?" Mrs. Wright asked, as she dashed frantically to the front door, peeking out a side window as Jim made his way upstairs, pulling June along with him.

"Jim! Hurry! They're almost here! Why did you open the gate!? You could have stalled!"

She had no time to think. No time to protest or ask questions. Jim forcefully tugged at her arm as they climbed the stairs, though she wasn't resisting. She nearly lost her footing several times as she tried desperately to keep up.

Once inside the pink bedroom, she watched as Jim frantically locked the door behind them. A feeling of helplessness consumed her as he pulled her into the walk-in closet, which his wife had so proudly showed off not even an hour before. Though she didn't intend to struggle, panic set in as he covered her mouth with his hand, leaving her gasping for air. The harder she tried to free herself, the tighter his grip became.

She felt as though the walls were rapidly closing in on her. She was hardly breathing by the time Jim decided to stuff some sort of fabric in her mouth. Her thoughts raced as she slipped in and out of consciousness. *Is it my parents!? Do they know I'm here?*

Sometime later, June slowly opened her eyes – seeing only the rows of clothing which hung just above her. Mr. Wright was nowhere to be found as she sat up cautiously. Her eyes burned as they adjusted to the light, her head pounding. She had no way of knowing how long she'd been out. *Could my parents still be here!?* Though she tried for several minutes, she found herself unable to stand.

It was then that she heard the sound of footsteps making their way into the bedroom. Within a few moments, she was faced with a distraught Mrs. Wright standing at the doorway of the closet, peering down at her.

"Goodness me, dear. Are you okay!?" she asked, a look of genuine concern on her tear-stained face. "Jim didn't mean it, honey. He just couldn't risk you screaming while the police were here."

This can't be real, she thought, burying her face in her hands.

"He was just so worried that… well, I know you're still confused, darling. He couldn't risk them taking you away."

"So, my parents sent them? They're looking for me?" she asked, her voice cracking with every word.

"Yes," she answered. "We expected they'd come by at some point… probably checking with all your friends too, to see if they know anything."

"They're looking for me," June said, her eyes welling with tears. "They're probably worried sick. Please… let me go home," she pleaded.

"No, dear. They're only doing what they feel they have to. They'll stop looking soon enough. Your home is here with us now."

She had no strength with which to oppose Mrs. Wright. Though she tried once more, she found herself unable to stand to her feet. Mrs. Wright quickly moved in to assist, with June having no choice but to accept the help. Her knees shook as she led her to the bed.

"I don't know that I'll be able to get you up on the bed, darlin.' That mattress is just so high off the ground," she said, leaning June gingerly against the side railing. "JIM!" she hollered loudly before June had the opportunity to protest.

He appeared within a matter of seconds, almost as if he'd been waiting in the hallway, she thought as she watched him enter the room. Though his demeanor was nothing short of casual, she found herself holding her breath as he walked toward her. She couldn't help but shudder as he wrapped his arm around her back to help her onto the bed, both remaining silent.

"Well, that's better!" Mrs. Wright said as she adjusted the light pink comforter. "Can I get you anything? Would you like some ice water?"

"No, I'm okay," June replied, avoiding eye contact.

"Jim, why don't you go ahead and set up that TV in here for her?"

She felt relieved at the opportunity to sit quietly for a while. She hated keeping up a façade with Mrs. Wright, who sat in the large chair next to the bed as they watched one of her hundreds of DVDs. She wondered how long they could sustain keeping an eye on her at all hours of the day and night. *Once they trust me again, they'll ease up… they have to.*

Though she couldn't remember most of the movie, it had been a welcome distraction from the current reality she faced. Her mind wandered as Mrs. Wright shared her thoughts on the film, to which she simply nodded politely in agreement.

"What about school?" June asked abruptly, clearly startling Mrs. Wright. She hadn't intended to blurt it out like that, but she couldn't help but wonder if this was something the Wrights had considered when electing to hold her captive.

"It's just that… I don't want to miss my senior year."

"Your education is very important to us, sweetie," she responded. "Jim and I had planned on talking to you about that soon and see what would be best for the family."

She felt an immediate lump in her throat. *The 'family'?*

"I'm sorry, Mrs. Wright… I just don't know what that means," she responded, trying her best to remain cordial.

"Goodness dear, please call me Roxie… And I just mean that it's something we'll need to discuss. I'm sure you understand that we can't stay in this town. Not with your parents here and all… lots of people that know you."

"We're moving?" she asked, though Mrs. Wright had already made it clear what they were planning.

"We are… but we want to include you in deciding where we go, June Bug."

Why does she call me that!? Only my dad calls me that!

"We can really go anywhere… is there somewhere you've always wanted to go?" she continued.

Are they planning to take me out of the country!? Do they really think that one day I'll be okay with this!?

"I don't know," she said, trying her best to keep from breaking down.

"I've already looked into some online programs for you. Shouldn't be a problem at all to knock out your senior year. In fact, we should start thinking about college soon."

Though she couldn't think of a response, June managed a nod of her head before Mrs. Wright had moved on to other topics of conversation.

Lunch was served on an antique wooden tray, which included a small vase of flowers from the garden. Though Mrs. Wright had ordered takeout Chinese food, which she'd sent her husband to fetch, June's lunch had been transferred to one of Mrs. Wright's dinner plates. It was as if her captors were trying to make amends for their wrongdoings, she thought as she did her best to eat. She knew she needed to get her strength back.

Mrs. Wright ate her own lunch in the chair next to the bed. June hated how she watched her every move, growing increasingly annoyed at her presence with every passing minute. She longed to be back in her own bedroom – reading a book, or just watching the ceiling fan spin above her head as she lay quietly in her bed.

If she has to be here, I might as well see what she'll tell me. Jim will never give up anything… but she doesn't think much before she speaks.

"I was wondering what the police said when they came by? Did they find my car?" she asked tentatively.

"They didn't say so. I doubt they've found it just yet," she replied, placing her own tray on the floor next to her. "They just wanted to know if we'd heard from you. Not much else they can do but ask around I expect, you being eighteen and all."

The idea that her parents may buy into the notion that she had simply run away caused her to feel pain in the pit of her stomach as she pushed her tray of food to the other side of the bed. *I mean, I did sneak out. This is my fault… why did I do that!? If the police think I ran away they aren't going to keep looking… she's right.*

"But you know… I didn't bring any extra clothes with me. Nothing but my purse and phone. I didn't bring *anything* else. Wouldn't they find that strange?"

"Maybe," she conceded, gathering June's tray as well as her own. "But you were angry, as you should have been. They'll likely chalk it up to just an impulsive decision… happens all the time with kids your age."

She knew for certain that the Wrights would not be letting her leave of their own accord. They had hoped she would stay with them willingly, but when that fell through, they seized the opportunity. Holding her captive was anything but an impulsive decision. The extent of their planning was nothing short of terrifying.

"Do you think you're up for a walk outside in a bit?" Mrs. Wright asked as she stood at the doorway, holding their lunch trays.

"Yes, I'd enjoy that," she answered warmly, masking her hatred for the woman she'd so recently considered a friend and confidante.

She was relieved to find it relatively easy to get moving again after lunch, despite having a bit of a shaky start getting out of bed. As they walked the grounds, Mrs. Wright chatted away as usual, commenting on everything from the flower garden to her distaste for the customer service at a local eatery. June shuddered as she noticed Jim standing next to the entryway gate, praying she wouldn't be forced to interact with him.

Apart from the Wrights, the only other person to have access in and out of the gate, to her knowledge, was Luca. Again she wondered if he could be in any way involved in their scheme. It seemed unlikely, but she was not in a position to rule anything out. She had trusted Mrs. Wright completely, and the consequences turned out to be catastrophic.

Fortunately, Mrs. Wright didn't stop to talk with her husband as they passed by the entrance. Though June had an especially hard time focusing on the current conversation, her interest peaked as she heard her captor mention the shutters, which she had asked Luca to paint.

"I sure do hope that color I chose will look as good as I imagined. Those shutters are in desperate need of a face lift. Should help the place sell quickly once we've moved on," she said coolly.

"Oh, I'm sure they will look great. When is he coming by to take care of that?" June asked, her mind racing as she tried to figure out how the Wrights planned to keep her from him. The only logical explanation for them allowing him on the premises whilst she was being held captive, she reasoned, was that he must be somehow involved.

"He'll be by in the morning. Kid doesn't work on Sundays... goes to church and all," Mrs. Wight said, making it seem as though a knock against him.

"Well… it will be nice to see him again," she said timidly.

"No, dear. I'm sorry, but he can't know that you're here. It's a bit of a risk having him out, but poor Jim just isn't very handy… can't manage everything on his own. We'll just have to keep you hidden. I *am* sorry."

Though she flinched at the thought of how her captors might ensure she stay both quiet and hidden, there was also a sense of relief. *Luca doesn't know anything.* It somehow made her feel better knowing that not *every* person she had met this summer was deceiving her.

"There's something else I wanted to talk about with you, Bug," she said, clearing her throat nervously. "I really wanted Jim to be here too, but he thought it might be easier on you just coming from me."

Though it was hard to imagine anything Mrs. Wright could have to say would surprise her at this point, she nodded politely as they walked along the massive privacy hedges near the back of the property.

"I know you're probably so confused by all of this, June. I would be, too. But there's a reason we did this, sweetheart. There's a reason we love you so much," she said, seemingly holding back tears. "Jim and I *did* lose our daughter at birth – that much is true," she continued, placing her hand on the small of June's back. "But she didn't pass away. We were still in high school, and our parents forced us to give her up. It wasn't our choice."

"Oh. I'm sorry to hear that, Mrs. Wright," she responded tentatively. Though she couldn't imagine what this could possibly have to do with *her*, she grew increasingly panicked with every passing moment.

"June, dear. The baby we gave up was Lorraine. It was your mother."

CHAPTER THIRTEEN

By the time she and Mrs. Wright had made their way back into the house, June felt as though the walls around her were spinning uncontrollably. There was nothing that could have prepared her for what Mrs. Wright had revealed as they walked the grounds of their massive estate. *It's not true. It can't be,* she thought, taking a seat in the living room. *She's insane. She'll say anything just to confuse me. She's a liar!*

She kept her head down as Mrs. Wright took a seat beside her.

"I know this doesn't make sense to you right now. You may not have even known that your mother was adopted," Mrs. Wright said, speaking a bit softer than usual.

"No, my mother wasn't adopted," she replied, finally looking up from her lap.

"Yes, honey. She was. In fact, for all the research we've done… Jim and I really have no way of knowing if Lorraine, herself, was ever told."

Though she tried to respond, she knew it to be a fruitless battle. She remained silent as Mrs. Wright placed her hand on her shoulder.

"I know that she lost her mother before you were even born… Eleanor, wasn't it? And Howard – he seems like a good man... I know you don't get to see him much."

Though her panic intensified with every word Mrs. Wright spoke, she managed to keep her composure. *How does she know their names!?*

"Sweetheart, they adopted your mother as a baby. But Jim and I... we are your biological grandparents."

Her cheeks grew warm as she tried desperately to hold back tears. "None of this could be true," she said, now looking squarely at Mrs. Wright. "If my mother is the baby that you and Jim gave up... then why... WHY do you hate her!?"

"I don't *hate* Lorraine," she responded, though seemingly a bit taken aback.

"All you do is attack her... it doesn't make any sense."

"Now, sweetie. You know that she's unfit to be a mother. You've told me so yourself."

"I didn't... you're twisting my words," she said, her voice shaking as she tried in vain to control her anger. "If she's your baby then WHY DO YOU HATE HER!?"

Though Mrs. Wright sat motionless, she never broke eye contact. "I don't hate her, sweetie. She's just not my baby anymore. You are."

"What are you talking about!?"

"I told you how we had that painting commissioned soon after Jim and I married. We didn't know what your mother looked like. All we had was the photo of her as a baby."

June nodded slightly, though still in disbelief that the photo she had discovered in Mrs. Wright's wallet could be that of her mother.

"We tried for many years to have another child, but it just didn't happen. I've stared at the little girl in that painting for decades now. And when I finally laid eyes on your mother this summer, I knew for certain that little girl was gone. Jim knew it too."

June flinched slightly as Mrs. Wright gently moved a strand of hair from her face.

"We looked for her a long time; we wanted to know her. But, needless to say, our focus has shifted," she said, patting her on the back as she spoke. "You're so innocent, sweetheart. Your mother... well, she's just... she's tainted. She has been tainted by life... by her experiences. It happens, I suppose."

"You said it yourself, Mrs. Wright – the little girl in that painting isn't real. She never was," she replied, her voice cracking.

"You're right about that... but that child... that child wearing pearls gave me *hope*, June. Hope that my girl would somehow make her way back to me one day."

"I'm sorry you were never able to know my mother – I really am," June said cautiously. "But she *did* grow up... and I can't replace what you lost. I've grown up, too."

"But don't you see, dear? That's the beauty of it. You're eighteen now. Your parents have no say-so. We can give you everything they can't."

"I *want* to live with my parents," she answered defiantly. "I can't stay here. You can't keep me locked up forever."

"Not forever, sweetie. You just need some time to adjust. Jim and I know you'll see it our way soon enough."

There was nothing more to say. She knew she wouldn't be talking her way out of this. They would never let her leave willingly. Her mind raced as she sat silently on the couch. Mrs. Wright had moved on to the kitchen, pouring juice in glasses and fixing a tray of snacks.

Though she tried to process the revelation that her captors may, in fact, be her biological grandparents, the idea seemed so improbable. *Wouldn't Mom have known if she was adopted? Did she just not tell me? Does Dad know? Why would she keep that from me!?*

"Could I go upstairs, please? I'm just really tired," she said, feeling more emotionally drained than physically.

"You want to take your drink upstairs? I can carry these snacks for you," she answered, her tone as warm as ever.

She didn't try to protest. Quarreling with Mrs. Wright would not better her current circumstances, she reasoned, as the pair made their way to the second story. Though every time she caught a glimpse of the front door her first instinct was to hit a dead sprint, she ultimately resisted. The Wrights were both in great shape, with Jim sporting a particularly athletic build for a man in his late-fifties. Despite that fact, June felt she had a decent chance at outrunning him, should it be necessary.

Weighing all factors in the balance, she knew her best bet would be to wait it out. *What if I try to run and get caught up at the gate? They'll probably lock me in the bedroom… or tie me up again.* She couldn't help but feel disappointed in herself at failing to control her anger in front of Mrs. Wright. The only way to get a step ahead of her captors would be to convince them that their plan was moving along.

"I almost forgot! I bought some things to keep you busy that I thought you might like," Mrs. Wright said as she quickly made her way to the bench at the foot of the bed. June watched as she carefully lifted the top, revealing stacks of colorful cardstock, various paints, glue, and canvases. There was also a small, wooden easel tucked away near the bottom of the bench. All the art supplies looked to be brand new, most still wrapped in plastic and sporting price tags.

"What do you think, dear?"

She couldn't help but think back to the day Mrs. Wright offered to lend a hand at redecorating their front window display at Randolphs. At the time, June found herself in awe of this woman who seemed so generous. It was still hard to believe how things had changed in a matter of weeks. Mrs. Wright had seemed, at the time, too good to be true. As it turned out, she *was*. It was all a rouse to win her over, and it had worked, she thought as she made her way over to the foot of the bed.

"This is great. Are you wanting me to make something in particular?" she asked, managing a slight smile.

"No, sweetie. Nothing in particular. I just know how creative you are. I'm not so sure you've had the chance to explore that creativity, what with you working all the time."

"I suppose that's true."

"I want you to be yourself here."

It was then that she heard footsteps, as Mr. Wright made his way upstairs.

"How's it going, ladies?" he asked, taking a seat in the chair next to the bed.

"Oh, just fine. June Bug and I've had a chance to talk and all. Now just showing her these art supplies I'd tucked away. Nearly forgot all about them."

"I see," he said, nodding his head as he glanced over at the mountain of paper, which sat dangerously close to the edge of the bed. "Glad you gals had a chance to talk things over."

"Oh, Jim! Do you have your phone on you? I wanted to show her some of those houses we were browsing the other day," Mrs. Wright said, never looking up from the cardstock she was busy stacking into neat piles.

Though she felt nothing short of terror at the thought of the Wrights taking her away, she managed to keep her composure as Jim reached into his pocket for his phone and handed it over to his wife.

"There is one in particular that I just know you'd love," Mrs. Wright said, grinning from ear to ear.

Where do they think they're taking me!? The thought had barely crossed her mind before Mrs. Wright shrieked with excitement, clearly having found what she was looking for. The image of a home nestled on a white, sandy beach appeared on the screen. Jim seemed well-versed in specifics of the home, reciting details such as the number of bedrooms and square footage, as his wife scrolled through interior photos.

As she gazed intently at each photo, hoping to discover any further clues as to the location of the residence, a message appeared on the screen. The text simply read, "Jim, this is Edward Randolph. Please give me a call back. Thanks."

Mrs. Wright hastily concealed the screen before handing the phone back to Jim.

"Has he been calling a lot?" June asked cautiously.

"Just once or twice since the police left. I expect they let him know what Roxie told 'em when they came by," he answered.

"Yes," his wife chimed in. "I told them we hadn't spoken since the last time you were over. Can't imagine what more there is to say."

"Will you call him back, Mr. Wright?"

"I wouldn't worry yourself with any of that, June. We've got it handled," he replied.

She knew that should she push any further they would only try to downplay the fact that her parents were actively searching for her.

"Sweetheart, you're safe now. I won't let your mother hurt you anymore," Mrs. Wright said in a way that made June feel as though her skin was crawling.

She remained silent, managing only a slight nod of the head. Though Roxanne's words dripped with hypocrisy, she could detect not the slightest hint of self-awareness. It seemed that she genuinely regarded Lorraine as the 'monster,' and herself as a savior of sorts.

"We've had so much fun together this summer. Now that doesn't have to end," she continued. "You'll want for nothing with us. I think you know that."

"I do," she said, forcing a contrived smile. "I'm sure it hasn't been easy… not being able to tell me who you are all this time."

"Well, you are right about that, sweetie," she replied, beaming from ear to ear. "But now you know!"

After carefully reorganizing the art supplies and removing various tags, Mrs. Wright returned the haul back into the bench before announcing that she needed to take a quick nap before dinnertime. Jim, of course, remained to keep watch of June.

"How's about a movie?" he asked, as his wife took her leave.

"Sounds good," she answered, dreading every minute.

Though she tried to focus her attention on the TV screen, she couldn't help but be distracted by Mr. Wright, who sat next to the bed. He clearly wasn't watching the movie either, as he'd been staring intently at his phone for several minutes. *Did my dad text him again?*

The Wrights clearly had the upper hand in the situation. Though she wanted only to sit in silence, she thought it imprudent to miss out on an opportunity to gain information. Though Jim wasn't typically much of a talker, she reasoned that it couldn't hurt to try.

"Jim, I was thinking about that day we met at the shop…" she said, breaking his focus.

"Oh, yeah…" he responded, an heir of suspicion in his voice.

"I just… I remember the way you reacted when you saw my mother. Of course, I didn't understand it at the time. I guess I'm just wondering why you seemed so stunned to see her… I mean, I just assume you'd been keeping up with us for quite a while. You knew you might see her when you came in the shop, right?" she asked, unintentionally holding her breath as she spoke.

Mr. Wright took his time before responding, clearing his throat and slipping his phone back into his pocket.

"Yeah, I knew I might see her that day. Thought I was prepared for it. Somehow it was still a bit of a shock to see her in person, I s'pose," he said, rubbing his forehead.

"But... you were fine talking to me."

"You're right about that. Of course, I knew I might see you too. It's difficult to explain, June. We barely had any time with her after she was born, but Roxie and I still felt like we knew her. Then when I finally saw her again... she just didn't live up to the idea I had in my head all these years."

SHE wasn't good enough for them!?

"I knew then for certain that *you* were the one we wanted," he continued.

She wanted nothing more than to scream at him. She wanted to defend her mother. She wanted to react to the sheer lunacy of his words, yet ultimately resisted.

"We gave up an innocent little girl, and that's what we wanted returned to us."

"So... how long ago did you find us?" she asked, her voice cracking a bit.

"Oh, it's been a few years I s'pose. We've kept up with all your accomplishments in school and all. Of course, we had to track down papers for all that. It's not as if your mama ever posted to social media about you," he said smugly. "We knew she might not be what we were looking for... though we didn't know how bad it really was until we met you all."

"What do you mean?"

"She doesn't seem to appreciate *you* too much, June… shouldn't that be explanation enough?"

"I guess that's true," she replied, albeit begrudgingly.

Though she wrestled with guilt at having contributed to their negative opinion of Lorraine, she knew that ultimately their shared psychosis ran much deeper than anything she could have been responsible for. Lorraine and Mrs. Wright's tense encounter at Randolphs weeks prior likely played a factor in solidifying their faulty beliefs, she thought as she sat quietly. *It's not a coincidence that they moved here now… right before my birthday. They thought they would convince me to live with them. They NEVER wanted Mom. They always wanted ME.*

"I think I understand, Jim… I do. But, you know, I *am* an adult now. You lost a baby, and I'm sorry, but… that's not something I can replace."

"We've watched you grow up for several years now, June… from afar. You may not feel like you really know us yet, but we know you," he said.

As the final credits rolled on the TV screen, Mrs. Wright reappeared, her mug of hot tea in hand.

"Who's hungry!?" she asked excitedly.

June smiled politely, though she couldn't imagine getting anything down after the conversation she had just endured with Jim. *They've really been keeping tabs on us all this time? Did they hire a P.I.? How does he know what Mom posts to social media? Do they have fake accounts?*

She couldn't help but feel sick as she considered how effortlessly they had been able to fool her. She thought of how they had manipulated her emotions, causing her to fall right into their con. She knew now that Mrs. Wright had leveraged the challenging relationship she had with her mother in order to sway her.

"I could eat," June said as she stepped foot off the massive bed in which she'd spent most of the day. "What are we having?"

Mrs. Wight had frozen several of the ready-made 'take and bake' casseroles from Jenny's Bistro, which June had all but forgotten mentioning to her days prior. She managed to engage in small talk over dinner. Mrs. Wright was as chatty as ever, clearly refreshed following her afternoon nap.

Though she felt certain that her captors' plan moving forward would be to manipulate her into, as they'd put it, seeing things 'their way,' she had a sense of peace knowing that this could never come to fruition. Mrs. Wright had exploited her weaknesses and betrayed her trust, and the time had come for June to do the same.

"Roxie, will you be keeping first watch over me tonight? I thought it might be fun to play a board game or something… if you're up to it. Mom has always hated that kind of thing, you know."

"Oh, sure! I have lots of games tucked away in the coat closet," she said, rising suddenly from the table. "We can play whatever you like, Bug. Though, I do need to get at least a few hours of sleep tonight.

Luca will be here bright and early to paint those shutters."

CHAPTER FOURTEEN

The next morning, June sat quietly in the pink bedroom as Mrs. Wright carefully placed plastic tablecloths along the floor. She'd arranged small paint bottles and brushes atop a nearby dresser earlier in the morning. An old, paint-splattered wooden easel belonging to Roxanne sat next to June's fresh art supplies. She couldn't help but roll her eyes as she set up her own easel, which still sported a price tag. *She thinks she can buy me off. Does she really believe that some paint and nice clothes will make me forget that I'm their prisoner!?*

"What do you think we should paint?" June asked, yawning. It wasn't easy getting to sleep with the Wrights keeping watch over her throughout the night. Mrs. Wright had relieved Jim from watch duty very early in the morning, in anticipation of Luca's arrival.

She had watched as Mrs. Wright closed both the blinds and curtains (which hung high above the bedroom window). She assumed they wanted to ensure that Luca would not be able to see her should he make his way to the backyard. *There's no way that Jim will let him in the house*, she thought, as Roxanne excitedly poured globs of paint onto two round pallets.

"Anything you want, dear! What would *you* like to paint?"

"I'm really not sure. I guess I'll just follow your lead," she replied warmly.

After wandering around a bit in the large, walk-in closet, Mrs. Wright emerged holding an emerald green dress with a jeweled neckline. The closet contained clothing items of all sorts in June's size. The green dress was relatively fancy, supporting her belief that the Wrights were expecting her complacency in their scheme to come relatively quickly, as this was not the type of garment to be worn just around the house. *They don't want to live this way forever. Once they trust me enough to take me somewhere, I can find help.*

"Jim plans on putting in an offer on that house we showed you," Mrs. Wright said, hanging the dress on the closet door. June's heart sank as she sat at the stool closest to her easel. *They will NEVER let me out of the house while we're still living here, no matter how much I can get them to trust me. Someone could recognize me.*

"It's a beautiful house. I'm sure it'd be nice to wake up next to the water every day," June said casually.

"Oh, of course it will! You and I can take walks along the beach. And I can't wait to get started decorating!" she replied, sitting at the stool next to June.

She knew the Wrights were intentionally keeping the *location* of the beach house from her. Though she didn't want to press the issue, she couldn't help but hope that perhaps Roxanne would unintentionally give something up.

"This dress is beautiful… though I can't imagine where I'd have to wear it."

"Well, once we're settled at the new house, I expect you'll have lots of chances to wear it, sweetie," Mrs. Wright replied, turning her attention to the white canvas sitting in front of her. "Now, how about we get to painting?" she asked excitedly. "I thought maybe this dress would be good inspiration for us."

It wasn't long after the pair began work on their respective canvases that she could hear as Jim made his way up the staircase. The thought of seeing him filled her with dread as she continued to mix colors, in an attempt to create the perfect emerald-green.

"Roxie, Luca is here," he said as he swung open the bedroom door.

"Okay, sweetie. We are just fine in here. If he needs me, you and I can switch out," his wife replied, barely taking the time to glance up at him.

"He's wanting you to take a look at the paint he bought before he gets to work," he said, making his way to the bench at the foot of the bed.

Mrs. Wright let out an audible sigh before placing her paint brush carefully onto her pallet. "I guess that's probably a good idea. Sometimes the colors look different than you were expecting," she said as she made her way out of the room. "Want to make sure the house will sell quickly once we've left."

They plan on us leaving before listing the house? It made sense they would want the house empty before it started to show, under the circumstances. Though she found herself a bit shaken, realizing the Wrights' plan to move them could be coming much sooner than anticipated, she managed not to react.

She had watched enough 'true crime' television over the years to understand that being moved to another location by her captors was less-than-ideal. Though, on the other hand, she would never be allowed to leave the Wrights' property while living so near to her home, no matter how much they'd grown to believe she had bought into their twisted way of thinking.

The closest connection she had to the outside world was Luca, who might as well have been a million miles away. She thought it ironic that Luca himself had installed the security camera at the front door. Unbeknownst to him, the camera likely aided the Wrights in keeping track of him while he tended to their property.

It then occurred to her that they likely had more than just the *one* security camera installed. She had never noticed others before, but then again, she simply hadn't paid attention. She glanced back at Jim who sat in silence behind her, before half-heartedly continuing work on her painting.

"That's lookin' good," he said after several minutes.

"Thank you. I used to take art classes when I was younger," she replied.

"Yeah, well… it shows. I dabbled in the arts myself. Guess you'd say I found my calling, though, in computers."

She smiled back at him before continuing to mix paints together on her wooden pallet.

"Of course, I can't *fix* a thing to save my life. Wish I could… but that's what we got Luca for. I've always found someone who could help me with house upkeep," he continued.

It seemed to her that Mr. Wright did, in fact, require a lot of help from Luca. Even chores as minor as changing out a lightbulb were delegated to their teenage employee. Though most of his time was spent tending to the landscaping, Roxanne required his help inside the house at least once a week, as she recalled.

She wondered if there was any scenario in which the Wrights might allow Luca to enter the home, should the need arise. *What if something breaks? Roxanne is so obsessive… she'd want it fixed.*

It was then that an antique perfume bottle caught her eye. It sat delicately atop the vanity next to her. The bottles varied in shape and color – all likely very expensive. She took a moment to admire the intricate detailing which appeared to be hand-painted.

June couldn't help but think of the Fenton glass back at home, though it was much different than the collection sitting before her. Nonetheless, the tiny flowers and vines reminded her of several of her mother's pieces, which were also hand-painted. The assortment of Fenton residing in their curio cabinet paled in comparison to that of Mrs. Wright's bottles of perfume, in terms of both rarity and value.

She felt ashamed in that moment of the resentment she had long held in regards to Lorraine's hobby. *How could I have been jealous of GLASS!? It's just something she enjoys… it never meant more to her than me.*

The vanity was equally as stunning as the glass collection in which it displayed, if not more so. The color was an antiqued off-white – particularly striking with the sunlight streaming in, which was currently nowhere in sight as both the blinds remained closed and drapes drawn shut. She noticed that the mirror was neither hanging above the piece, nor was it leaning against the wall. It seemed as though it was attached to the bottom portion, likely via screws. *Could I break it? Would they let Luca in here to fix it!? Maybe I could leave a note for him!?*

It wasn't long before Mrs. Wright returned, allowing Jim to head back outdoors with Luca.

"Well, good news… that color I picked for the shutters is even prettier in person," Mrs. Wright said as she resumed work on her painting. "Looks like you're coming along quite nicely in here."

"Yes. This was a great idea," she replied. "Of course, I do wish we could open up the blinds. It'd be nice to have some natural light in here."

"Well, I can't argue with that, sweetie. But we just can't risk Luca seeing you while he's here."

"Right. I understand," she responded casually. "Just… I really don't think that if we opened them just a bit that anyone could see through this window… especially with it being so high."

She watched as Mrs. Wright directed her gaze at the closed drapes behind them. "Well, I suppose you're right. And it really would be nice to have some more light in here," she said. "Luca's in the front yard anyhow. Why don't you go open the blinds just a bit…

and leave a little gap in the drapes? Them things are so heavy… I'm looking forward to shopping for some new ones for the beach house. Jim and I figure we'll leave a lot of this stuff behind."

Pulling the drapes back slowly afforded June the opportunity to examine the side of the vanity, which sat within arm's reach from the window. She glanced back at Mrs. Wright every few seconds, paranoid that she might catch on to her scheming. *How could I get those screws loose? Where would they even keep a screw driver? The garage?*

She knew that it would need to appear as if unintentional. Should the Wrights suspect she had tampered with the piece herself, it would only set her back.

"That's perfect, dear," Mrs. Wright said, turning to look back at her.

"Yes. That helps a lot," she replied before making her way back to her seat.

"How about I bring you up a tray once we're done here? I know Jim will be wanting to eat soon."

Sometime later, Mrs. Wright made her way downstairs, with Jim taking over watch duty. Though she made a concerted effort to engage him in small talk, her mind inevitably wandered back to the vanity. She hadn't managed to get a good look at the screws which held the piece together. Although she had never considered herself to be particularly handy, she'd picked up basic home maintenance skills from her father over the years.

I'll never get a hold of a screw driver, she thought, watching as Jim peeked cautiously through the bedroom window blinds. *Even if I did, they'd have to leave me alone in here for there to be time to loosen the screws.* Her first priority had to be to gain their confidence. Without it, she knew she'd never make it out before the move.

"How are the shutters coming along, Mr. Wright?"

"Oh, just fine. I thought they were alright the way they were, myself. But, you know, that's Roxie's jurisdiction."

It was then that Mrs. Wright entered the room, a tray of food in tow. "Did I hear my name, Jim?" she asked playfully.

"Yes ma'am. We were just in here discussing your good taste," her husband replied with a grin.

"Sweetie, your plate is on the kitchen table," she said, placing the tray in front of June.

"Are you eating up here?" he asked before heading out the door.

"Oh, I'll eat mine a bit later. I'm not too hungry at the moment. Happy to just sit with my girl here."

Mrs. Wright seemed less talkative than usual as June sat eating her meal, which included two different types of tea-sized sandwiches.

"Are you okay, Roxie?"

"Oh, right as rain. I just have a lot on my mind, I suppose. But I couldn't be happier that you're finally home with us for good."

June nodded before taking another bite of pasta salad from her plate.

"In fact, Bug. I've got something for you," she said, reaching into her pocket. "It's from Jim and I both. It's something we've saved for many years."

She smiled as she reached for the small, velvet drawstring bag that Mrs. Wright offered her. June had admittedly grown quite fond of Roxanne's gifts. Though that fact was now merely a source of shame and regret, her constant doting had an undeniable impact on June's willingness to let her guard down with a complete stranger. She had been fooled with nothing more than boutique clothing and costume jewelry, she thought as she opened the bag.

Inside the bag was a beautiful pearl necklace. She knew it to be a very high-dollar piece, as it sported large, white pearls.

"We bought this about the time we had that painting done. Somehow, I never stopped believing she'd find her way back to us," Roxanne said, staring at the portrait hanging just above the bed.

"It must have been hard... not knowing where she was all those years," June replied.

"Yes, it was."

She noticed Mrs. Wright's gaze shift to the string of pearls she held in her hand as she spoke. "You know, childhood is just so fleeting. And children, well... they're impressionable."

"That's true," June quietly responded.

"When we finally found Lorraine, well… like we've told you, I had always pictured giving these to a little girl. A child that had been our missing piece all these years," she said, tears streaming down her face.

"They're beautiful, Roxie. Thank you," she said, patting Mrs. Wright's hand.

She thinks I'm an impressionable child. They think I'll just mold into whomever they want me to be.

"Well, look at me over here making a fool of myself," she said, wiping her face. "Let's try it on you."

She realized at that moment she was still wearing the locket which her parents had gifted her days prior. She could see that Mrs. Wright was paying attention as she placed her hand to the charm.

"Would you like me to put that over on the vanity for you, sweetie?"

She couldn't help but feel that this was some sort of test. A test of her emotional attachment to something her parents had given her, perhaps?

"Sure," she replied, working to undo the clasp.

She didn't *want* to take it off. In a way, she felt as though Mrs. Wright was trying to strip her of her true identity, little by little. She hated the idea of accepting *anything* from the Wrights ever again. She loathed every moment spent playing along with their bizarre delusions. But she also knew, *it's the only way.*

The length was more like that of a choker than a typical necklace, she thought as Mrs. Wright secured the clasp behind her. Though, as Mrs. Wright said herself, it had been purchased for a young child.

"Well, now! Don't you look stunning, my dear. Such the fashionista with your new haircut and pearls."

"Thank you. It really is beautiful," she replied.

She then spotted the wooden food tray still sitting on the bed beside her. Something underneath the dinner plate suddenly caught her eye, which she had failed to notice earlier. It looked to be a small knife.

She could only assume that Mrs. Wright had used the knife to cut her sandwiches, forgetting to remove it before delivering the tray. Roxanne served most every meal on large, fancy dinner plates with ornate rims. It wasn't surprising that she *could* have missed it. *But what if this is another test? Did she leave it there on purpose?*

"They just suit you so well… like they were made for you," Mrs. Wright gushed. It seemed as if Roxanne's warped sense of reality had been exponentially validated by the mere sight of June wearing the pearls.

It was then that she heard the distant sound of a chime, followed quickly by the slamming of a door. She had heard that same chime dozens of times before. Every time either a door or window had been opened at the home, it inevitably sounded. She reasoned that she must have started tuning it out after spending so much time there, as she hadn't paid it any attention since being taken captive. *It's an alarm system. Of course they have an alarm!*

"Guess Jim went to check on Luca, the poor dear. I hope he brought himself enough water for the day."

"Yeah. I hope so, too."

Why didn't I pay attention to any of this? I don't even know if they have more than just the one camera.

As she slid her hand carefully towards the knife, she kept her eyes fixated on Mrs. Wright, who had just turned her attention to her cell phone.

"I think I might have Jim bring me up a plate after all," she said, seemingly crafting a text.

June knew that the cards were stacked against her. She'd be lucky to make it out of her bedroom, let alone the house should she try and plan an escape. She needed more time. Time to convince Jim and Roxanne that she wouldn't try to leave. Time to plan. *What if this really is a trick to see if I'll take it? Can I risk that? Could she really be that careless?*

"Did you have enough to eat?" Mrs. Wright asked, glancing briefly up at her.

"I did, thank you," she replied, carefully grabbing hold of the knife.

I'd never make it out of here with JUST this. I can't fight. Would I really be able to hurt them if it came down to it? Her mind raced as she kept her eyes squarely on Mrs. Wright, who had seemingly failed to notice she now had the knife in hand. *But maybe I could use this to loosen the vanity's screws. They may let Luca in here to fix it. I could leave a message for him behind the mirror... or something.*

"How'd you like that chicken salad sandwich? Was it any good?" Roxanne asked, never taking her eyes off her phone.

Maybe I'm being stupid. I should just run NOW! And if I have to use the knife, I will. I'm their prisoner! They kidnapped me! Jim could have killed me in that closet. There's no telling what they'll do!

"Oh yeah, the chicken salad… it was good," she replied. "Mrs. Wright…"

"Yes, dear?"

"I think you forgot this," she said, presenting the knife in her outstretched hand, offering it gingerly to her captor.

CHAPTER FIFTEEN

"Sweetheart! Why don't you come down for lunch?"

"Yes, ma'am," June replied, folding a page of her book. As she made her way down the grand staircase, she smelled the aroma of chicken and dumplings as it permeated the house. It was one of her favorite meals.

"I had Jim pick it up. Thought you might like to have it one last time before we leave," Mrs. Wright said as she fixed their plates.

"Thank you. Looks great," she said, smiling as she took a seat at the kitchen table. "Is Jim eating?"

"Oh, he'll have some a bit later I'm sure. He's outside with Luca right now."

"How long has he been here? I completely forgot that today is Saturday."

"Not too long. Tuesday will be his last day while we're still here. I need you to help me to remember to make him a list," she said while serving June her lunch. "It's just a few little things I need him to do. The house is pretty much ready to be listed, just as soon as we've hit the road!"

"It looks great," she responded, taking a bite of dumpling.

"I still can't imagine why it took so long for us to close on the beach house… especially with it being a cash offer," Mrs. Wright said, rolling her eyes. "Oh well, at least it finally happened… you're going to love it!"

"I know it. I'm excited to see my new room. Could we go shopping once we've made it?" June asked.

"Oh, of course, dear! We're going to do it up right. You know I wouldn't let the house stay bare for long," Mrs. Wright replied with a grin.

"Will Luca need to fix anything inside today? I'm happy to stay in my room. I've got a book I need to finish anyway."

"Well, truth be told, there are a few things I need him to take care of… but, you know, Jim is trying to have him wait on those until we're gone. He's still not comfortable having him in the house with you here."

"*You* know I don't want anyone finding me, don't you?" she asked as Mrs. Wright filled their glasses with tea.

"Of course, sweetie. And Jim knows it too. He's just still a bit cautious. We've kept prying eyes away for a whole month, and we don't want anything going awry now that we've made it to the home stretch," Mrs. Wright responded. "We've just been so happy… the three of us."

"Yes. We have," June said warmly, patting Mrs. Wright on the hand.

It had been just over a month since she was first taken captive by her biological grandparents, Jim and Roxanne Wright. She felt certain that she had succeeded in convincing them that she was now acquiescent in their scheme. Though they maintained certain safeguards to ensure that she was unable to leave the premises, they had significantly loosened the proverbial 'reigns.'

The Wrights no longer insisted upon keeping watch of her every minute of every day. She was allowed to roam the house relatively freely, though spent most of her time alone in the pink bedroom. She relished the time she had to herself to read or watch movies. Jim even allowed her to sleep alone in the bedroom at night, though he and his wife alternated keeping post in the hallway, just outside her door. She felt that this was largely just for show, as she would inevitably hear the sound of snoring a mere hour or so after she had turned in for the night. Mrs. Wright had set up a small cot in the hallway once they deemed it safe to allow her privacy as she slept.

June knew they were trying to win her over as best they could. They no longer discussed anything having to do with her parents, nor the fact that they were holding her there against her will. It was as if they wanted her to forget everything that had transpired mere weeks prior.

She, in turn, did her best to convince them that their plans were coming to fruition – that she had, in fact, bought into it. She had them believing that she was excited to move to the 'beach house,' as they called it, though its exact location remained a mystery to her. She no longer asked questions which might bring about suspicion that she desired to leave. She even indulged Mrs. Wright when asked to try on various outfits and accessories from her fully-stocked closet.

Though they made certain to close all blinds and curtains before Luca arrived to take care of the property, she was no longer required to stay in the pink bedroom for the entire duration of his time there. Tuesday was his day to mow the yard, pull weeds, and edge the driveway. Saturdays were reserved for trimming hedges, and any other projects Mr. Wright had for him. June wondered if Luca found it strange that she had suddenly vanished, though she didn't dare to ask Roxanne if he had asked about her.

She still had no access to local television stations, so it was impossible to know whether or not her disappearance had been publicized in any way. Should the police have concluded that she was merely an eighteen-year-old 'runaway,' there was likely no mention of it in the press. Though she felt certain that her parents were, in fact, looking for her despite what the Wrights would have her to believe.

She had spent most of her time the past several weeks quietly taking note of all the daily ins-and-outs of the home in which she found herself. The house was equipped with a fairly extensive security system, as June had come to realize. The video camera near the front door was only one of six, which were mounted along the exterior of the house, not including the one at the front entrance gate. All of the doors and ground-floor windows would 'chime' when opened during the day, though not the second-story windows. It was part of Jim's nightly routine to set the alarm system before bed.

June had gained the Wrights' confidence, at least to a certain degree. She didn't intend to allow them to take her to the beach house. The time had come for her to make a move. It was time to get herself out.

Three days later, she folded clothes as Mrs. Wright excitedly taped up large moving boxes. Roxanne had recruited her to help with packing up the house as moving day drew near. They had started with Jim and Roxanne's shared closet, and had moved on to June's early that morning.

"Once we've finished up in here, why don't we get started in the kitchen? I just have so many utensils and all. I really just need to donate a lot of it," her captor said as she grabbed a stack of neatly-folded sweaters.

"Sure. Has… Luca been by yet this morning?" June asked cautiously.

"Oh, yeah. He's here. I think Jim's out there with him already. It'd be nice if that man of mine could help with some of this packing," she said, playfully rolling her eyes.

She needed some time alone in her bedroom. She hadn't planned on Mrs. Wright getting started on packing so early in the morning. Though she knew that Tuesday was typically a long day of work for Luca, she couldn't help but shudder at the thought of missing him before he'd left. *How can I get her to leave me alone in here?*

"Umm… Roxie. I know we have a lot to get done today, but I'm just not feeling my best. Would you mind if I lie down for a little while?"

"Well certainly, Bug. What is it that's bothering you?" she asked, seeming concerned.

"I'm just really tired today. I didn't get a lot of sleep last night… and my stomach has been bothering me a bit."

"Goodness. Yes, of course. You just rest up as long as you need to today. I've got the packing under control. You know, it might just be that you're nervous about the move. I know it's a lot of change for you. But I'm certain you'll just love it," she said, covering June in her pink comforter.

"You might be right. I think I just need to relax for a bit."

"Sure. I'll check on you later," Roxanne said, closing the door behind her.

Though she took a few moments to lay quietly under the covers, for fear that Mrs. Wright may return and catch her out of bed, she felt anything but relaxed. Her anxiety was palpable as she gently placed her hand to her neck. She had worn the string of pearls the Wrights had gifted her every day of the past month, terrified to take it off.

She had often found herself carefully studying the portrait which hung above her bed. She knew it was meant to represent her mother, yet she saw no glimpse of Lorraine Randolph staring back at her. The child in pearls was merely an idealized version of the baby the Wrights had given up as teenagers. It was now June, herself, whom they idealized. They had placed her on their own psychotic pedestal, and were willing to keep

her there by any means necessary. *June* was now their
real-life child in pearls.

Several minutes passed before she heard the
clanging of pots and pans in the kitchen, indicating that
the coast was clear. She had spent the previous night
painstakingly bending one of the prongs of a lamp plug
so that she might utilize it as a makeshift screw driver.
She had managed to bend it back far enough to where it
wouldn't hinder her use of the unaltered prong.

Making her way over to the vanity, she noticed
her hands shaking slightly at her sides. After gently
placing the lamp on the hardwood floor, she carefully
pulled back the curtains to give herself as much light to
work with as possible, without opening the blinds. Her
stomach turned as she retrieved a marker from the
collection of art supplies which Mrs. Wright had given
her. She found it difficult to keep her hand steady as
she quickly inscribed a message onto the backside of
the vanity mirror.

Sweat poured down June's face as she loosened
the final screw which held the heavy, oversized mirror
onto the vanity. She had spent the past half-hour
working diligently on the piece of furniture, which she
knew to be her one and only hope of getting in contact
with Luca.

She stopped short of removing any of the
compromised screws. Though she felt confident that
Jim would make no attempt at fixing the piece himself,
it needed to appear as if accidental. She couldn't risk the
mirror itself breaking, as she thought it unlikely
Roxanne would take the time to have new glass cut

before their move. It needed to be something easy. It needed to be something Luca could fix.

She pushed the left side of the mirror backwards in such a way that it dropped several inches behind the desk portion of the vanity, though remaining secure enough so not to fall off completely. She could only pray that it would appear to the Wrights as though the antique mirror was simply showing its age, thus in need of some attention before being placed in a moving truck. *What if they just want to get rid of it? Mrs. Wright said we'd be leaving a lot behind.*

"Roxie!" June shouted from the banister. She had reached a point of no return, which felt strangely just as comforting as it was terrifying.

"Do you need me, Bug?" Mrs. Wright quickly responded.

"Yes. I'm so sorry. I was feeling better so I sat at the vanity to fix my hair… I think I may have broken it."

Mrs. Wright made her way up the steps, seemingly worn down from her morning spent packing boxes.

"Oh, I doubt it," she said, appearing as if unconcerned.

"I leaned my arm against the top of it as I was opening up the curtains… then I heard a 'pop.'"

"I see," Mrs. Wright said, inspecting the damage. "It's very old… I'm not surprised, really."

"I know it is. I don't know what I was thinking," she responded, as though remorseful.

"Don't fret, dear. This thing is dreadfully heavy anyway. We can get you a more modern one for your new room."

"Oh, but... I just love this vanity. It's such a beautiful piece... and I'd feel so guilty if we had to leave it behind because of me."

Mrs. Wright sighed. "That's true. I *have* had it with me for quite a long time. Let me talk to Jim and we'll see what he says."

June couldn't help but to feel a bit panicked as she sat at the edge of the bed, anxiously awaiting Mrs. Wright's return. *He'll never go for it. He hasn't let Luca step foot in the house since I've been here. Now what will happen when the vanity gets moved? They'll know I was trying to escape. It'll make everything so much worse!*

The sound of Roxanne making her way up the staircase left her with an overwhelming feeling of dread. *This is my one shot. It's the last time Luca will be here before we move... what if Jim won't let him in to fix it?*

"Alright, sweetie. Why don't you and I head to my room? We can take a board game or two with us if you like," she said, opening the door.

"Jim is... having Luca fix the mirror?" June asked tentatively, inadvertently holding her breath as she spoke.

"Yes. It shouldn't take Luca too long. I'm sure it's an easy fix that we wouldn't want to make worse by trying to move the thing. To tell you the truth, I think

Jim may even be a little attached to that vanity; we've had it so long."

She managed to keep her excitement suppressed as she and Roxanne made their way down the hallway. Her elation, however, soon turned to panic. She and Mrs. Wright had just begun their fourth round of 'Go Fish' when she realized there was something she hadn't considered. *How will I know if Luca sees the message!? I should have just taped a note to the back instead... then I could see if it was gone. I won't know if he's coming tonight or not!*

CHAPTER SIXTEEN

June stared out the window of her second-story bedroom. Attempts to make out anything located in the Wrights' backyard seemed futile, as it was currently pitch black and eerily still. Her only source of light in the bedroom was the television, which displayed a digital clock in a corner of the screen while idle. *Five more minutes. He'll be here*, she thought, making a conscious effort to keep breathing.

The home's alarm system was very sophisticated. Though she knew for certain that her bedroom window did not 'chime' when opened during the day, her hands still shook as she carefully pulled back the small latches which kept it locked. *It's not wired. The alarm won't sound.*

She could only assume that it wouldn't be seen as necessary to arm upstairs windows, as it would be unlikely for someone to try to break into a home from the second story. She couldn't help but appreciate the irony of the fact that while most alarms serve to keep others out, the Wrights' system served primarily to keep her *in*.

She breathed a sigh of relief as she slowly opened the window, feeling the outside air as it rushed into the bedroom. The alarm did not sound. Though she moved as quietly as possible, the old window still creaked as it was lifted. She wished there was *something* for her to grab hold of outside the window. A tree branch, or even just a lower ledge would be nice, she thought as she gazed out into the darkness. There was nothing but a straight shot to the concrete below – absolutely no way to escape.

Mr. Wright lay sleeping on the cot just outside June's bedroom door, leaving his wife the master to herself. It had been nearly two weeks since Roxanne had taken a 'night shift.'

She stopped to listen for the sound of Jim's snoring at least every thirty seconds, praying she wouldn't wake him. Most nights she found the earsplitting noises annoying as she tried to get to sleep herself. However, on this particular evening she welcomed it gladly. Glancing back at the clock, she felt a sudden lurch in the pit of her stomach. It was eleven P.M. on the dot. *It's time.*

She wore a casual shirt, which she'd tucked into a pair of jeans, both of which had come from the closet which Mrs. Wright had stocked. She hadn't seen the clothes she wore when first taken captive since that day. She had placed them in the bathroom hamper, but they were never returned. She wondered if Mrs. Wright was either consciously or unconsciously trying to eliminate anything which might spark memories of the night she was tied to the bed post, terrified and sobbing. Thankfully, June's white, Converse sneakers had managed to remain on the floor of the walk-in closet for the past month. She quickly checked to make sure her laces were tied tightly.

She ran her hand along the smooth surface of one of the antique perfume bottles, which sat atop the vanity next to the window. She grabbed one bottle in each hand, pausing for a brief moment to admire their beauty.

After taking one final deep breath, she forcefully hurled the bottle which she held in her right hand onto the concrete below. The sound of glass shattering disrupted the calm of the night even more so than she had anticipated. One by one, she launched the bottles out the window.

It only took a few moments before Jim began to stir on the other side of the door. She was counting on him running out the back, as the patio was where the commotion was coming from. She listened as his feet hit the hardwood floor, though she continued rapidly grasping at bottles to throw.

Within about thirty-seconds of the first bottle breaking, she heard as Jim made his way quickly, and loudly, down the staircase. This was her chance. She knew the time had come, and there was no turning back. Forcefully swinging open the bedroom door and sprinting down the steps, the alarm system rang out loudly as Jim had clearly made it out into the backyard.

Her eyes fixated on the front door as she made her way closer and closer. *I'll make it. I will.* She heard as Jim called out for Roxanne through the deafening sound of the siren. *She'll run out the back, too. I'll have time to make it to Luca!*

The only source of light downstairs was that of Mrs. Wright's candles, which sat burning on a narrow entryway table. The woman loved her candles, and kept them burning constantly around the house. June was relieved to find they made it a bit easier for her to see the front door as she quickly unlocked the deadbolt and rushed out into the night.

Breathing in the night air, it felt almost as if none of what was happening was real. She had made it out the front door. She could see next-to-nothing in front of her as she hit a dead sprint. *Luca is here. I know he is! He'll keep his lights turned off until he sees me.*

June had never seen herself as being particularly bold. She generally liked to play it safe, finding comfort in those things which were familiar. It wasn't often that she found herself faced with situations which required a significant shift from her reserved demeanor.

Ethan Morris and his friends' antics at the shop earlier in the summer had forced her out of her typical persona, if only for a day. Her less-than-ideal relationship with her mother had finally come to a head when she defied her parents, disrupting the status quo of the family. Though she wasn't proud of *every* decision she'd made the past couple of months, she could still acknowledge the growth that had taken place. She was *changing*. She was growing into the person she had always known herself to be.

She had been held against her will, physically and emotionally abused by a couple she falsely believed to be her friends. She had been fooled, manipulated, and groomed by two very sick individuals. Though she knew logically that the blame lay solely with the Wrights, she couldn't help but to feel in some way responsible.

She knew she couldn't let them win. They couldn't have her. She *had* to make it out.

She told herself not to look back as the sound of the alarm pierced through the calm of the night. *Where is he!? He HAS to be here!* She couldn't see if the gate was open or closed – it was just too dark.

She slowed to a jog, desperately hoping to spot Luca's truck. The Wrights' massive driveway was very wide, and she worried she might run past him should he be parked on the opposite side. She could barely see mere feet in front of her, narrowly avoiding tripping over a large crack in the concrete.

Where is he!? He's not here! He didn't see my message. They're going to kill me! I have to make it over the gate. I have to GET OUT!

CHAPTER SEVENTEEN

She couldn't catch her breath. *Where is he!?* Tiny rocks skidded across the driveway as she ran. *He can't see me! It's just too dark.* She felt suddenly lightheaded and weak. Panic was starting to set in. She couldn't find Luca. She had no way of knowing if he was even there waiting. The Wrights could discover her absence at any moment, if they hadn't already.

It was then that a flash of light lit up the drive, though only for a brief second. It was him. Luca had flashed the headlights of his truck. It had come from the opposite side of the driveway. *Did he see me?* A rush of emotion consumed her as she ran, sprinting toward the direction of the light. *I'll make it!*

Headlights flashed once again, illuminating the driveway as she grew nearer. Luca was the only person apart from the Wrights who knew the code to the front entrance gate. *Almost there. Almost there.*

June estimated she was mere feet from Luca's truck before being suddenly knocked to the pavement. Someone had thrown their body against hers, causing a violent crash. She could see that it was none other than Mrs. Wright who lay on top of her, violently trying to pin her arms as she struggled to get free.

"She's here! Jim! I've got her! Help me!" Mrs. Wright yelled frantically into the night.

June tried to block out the pain as Mrs. Wright grabbed onto her arms, which were bloodied and raw.

"GET OFF!" June yelled as she tried rolling over her body, in an effort to loosen her grasp.

"JIM! She's getting loose! JIM!"

The sound of shoes hitting the concrete grew louder and louder.

"Jim, we're here!"

Mrs. Wright shrieked as she was suddenly rushed by Luca, causing her to lose her grasp on June. She was free, and Luca had quickly neutralized Mrs. Wright, pinning her to the ground.

"June! Get in the truck!" Luca yelled as Mrs. Wright buried her long fingernails into his arm.

"JIM!" she yelled. "She's getting away!"

June quickly threw open the passenger-side door of Luca's truck. The engine was still running. She could see that Mrs. Wright was no match for Luca, despite her relentless attempts to claw violently at his skin.

She needed to get to him. Without thinking, she made her way over the middle console and into the driver's seat. She flipped on the headlights before pressing her foot to the gas pedal. Though it took mere seconds to make it to them, she couldn't seem to get there fast enough.

"Luca! Get in! Get in!" she yelled, praying that Mrs. Wright would be unable to immediately follow after him once released. She watched as he quickly let go of her arms and darted toward the passenger-side door. *We're going to make it!*

There was a sudden, deafening sound as Luca violently hit the ground just beside the truck. June sat speechless as he lay mere feet from her, blood pouring down his face. Jim stood towering over him, yielding a baseball bat which was now pointed directly at June. As he opened the door and pulled her from the vehicle, she could do nothing but comply.

She felt as though in utter shock as she stared at Luca's limp body, which seemed as if unreal. He wasn't moving. She couldn't tell if he was even breathing. *I turned on the headlights. That's how Jim found us. I did this. It's my fault. He's dead. Jim killed him, and now he's going to kill me too.*

"Get inside, Roxie," Mr. Wright barked as he dragged June along with him toward the house.

She could see that Mrs. Wright was slowly standing to her feet, even taking a moment to dust herself off before following behind them.

"Where were you, Jim!? How did Luca know she was here!?"

Mr. Wright refused to acknowledge his wife's line of questioning as they made it through the front door. Upon entering the foyer, June was shoved to the ground. The back of her head slammed against the bottom step of the grand staircase.

She was bruised and in pain. Both dirt and fragments of pavement stuck to the blood which covered both her arms and face. Her head throbbed as she painstakingly made her way back onto her feet. She kept one arm draped around the banister in an effort to keep herself upright, as the room was now spinning.

"You made a mistake, girl," Jim said, still standing at the front door, which remained open. "Now, I'm going to have to make sure that boy out there isn't going to wake up again," he said, pointing behind him.

"No, please. It's not his fault," she said, now sobbing uncontrollably.

"Sweetheart, where are your pearls?" Mrs. Wright asked, as if they were all sitting together over breakfast.

"Wha… what?" she questioned, doubting seriously that she had heard Roxanne correctly.

"You're not wearing the pearl necklace we gave you."

June slowly raised her hand to her neck, where she then grasped the locket which her parents had given her.

"I left it upstairs," she answered, without shame or hesitation.

"Why would you do that? Why would you try to leave us?" Mrs. Wright asked, staring intently.

"This is *not* my home. You are *not* my mother. And I am *not* the little girl in that painting. I never will be," she answered, never taking her hand off the locket. "You can't have me, Mrs. Wright."

"Your parents don't love you, June. They never have. Jim and I are the only ones who care about what happens to you," Mrs. Wright responded as she made her way toward her.

"That's not true," she said, her eyes once again welling with tears.

"Don't worry, Roxie. She'll never get loose again," Jim interjected. "I have to take care of this kid in my driveway now," he said as he made his way toward June who still stood at the base of the staircase. "I'll help you get her tied up first." June winced as he grabbed a fist-full of her thick hair.

It was then that she saw Luca standing at the front door, though hardly recognizable through the blood, dirt, and swelling of his face. He held Mr. Wright's baseball bat in his right hand, which had been left on the porch.

It was mere seconds before she found herself, once again, lying flat on the ground. All she knew for certain was that Luca had started swinging. She felt as Roxanne wrapped her arms quickly around her torso and pulled her up off the cold floor. She was trying to drag her up the steps, away from Luca and Mr. Wright.

"Let go of me! Let go!" June screamed loudly, clawing at her face. She couldn't see Luca. She couldn't see Jim. She could only hear the sound of their struggle as she finally freed herself from Mrs. Wright.

As she quickly wiped hair and sweat from her eyes and glasses she could see as Luca took yet another blow at Mr. Wright, who was seemingly trying to make it to his office, which was right off the foyer. *He may have a knife in there, or a gun!*

"Luca! Luca, just run! Let's run!"

She darted toward him. "Let's run!" she repeated before pulling at his free arm. She knew she had crashed into something in her haste to retrieve Luca, but never stopped. Mrs. Wright shrieked loudly behind her as the smell of smoke filled the air.

June had inadvertently knocked the narrow entryway table to the ground, including several of Mrs. Wright's still-burning candles. Jim stopped dead in his tracks as June managed to pull Luca toward the front door.

The foyer was quickly filling with smoke as the flames spread rapidly. The pair had nearly made it to the front door before Mrs. Wright slammed it shut.

"You're not leaving!" she shouted, blocking the door with her body.

"Get out of the way!" June cried, attempting to shove her away from the door.

The fire had now spread throughout the entryway around them. Jim stomped rapidly at the ground, though his attempts to quash the flames proved futile. His breathing grew increasingly labored and heavy before he started to cough uncontrollably.

"Let us out! We're all going to die!" June shouted at Mrs. Wright, who was fighting them tooth and nail.

The room grew hazy. June's head began to throb, with both she and Luca now coughing as they continued to struggle with Mrs. Wright.

Though she was clearly struggling to breathe, Roxanne proved immovable in her efforts to keep them from the door. Her face grew increasingly pale with every passing moment. She once again dug her long nails into June's arms as they struggled. It was then that June spotted the baseball bat, which lay mere feet from them.

"Move! Now! Or I WILL hit you!" she screamed, grabbing the bat from the floor.

Mrs. Wright's expression had finally turned to a look of utter defeat as she stared squarely at June, who now held the bat behind her head, ready to swing. Jim had collapsed onto his hands and knees near the office, hardly breathing.

"All I ever did was love you, June," Mrs. Wright said, her skin now alarmingly discolored.

"You're wrong. This isn't love," she said, adjusting her grip on the bat, ready to strike.

Mrs. Wright maintained eye contact with June for one final moment before suddenly making her way over to Jim, vacating her post.

"Let's go!" Luca said as he threw open the front door, pulling June along with him. As they reached the front porch, she turned to see that Jim had made it back onto his feet, assisted by his wife. Though Luca had left the front door open, the Wrights had failed to emerge by the time she and Luca made it back to his truck.

"Do you think they made it out the back door?" June asked as Luca hastily adjusted the gearshift and peeled out into the night.

"I don't know," he answered, constantly wiping sweat and blood from his face. He was clearly in a lot of pain.

She breathed a sigh of relief as they made their way out of the front entrance gate.

It felt somehow surreal to be sitting there next to Luca. She had not spoken to a single person apart from her captors for a month. In a way, she had doubted she would ever have the chance to speak to Luca, her parents, or anyone else she cared about ever again.

"Why didn't you want me to call the police?" he asked, referring to the message she had inscribed on the back of the vanity.

"The first time the police showed up... Jim nearly killed me," she said, keeping her eyes on the road ahead. "I think he would have succeeded this time. They were never going to let me go."

Luca then reached for her still-shaking hands. Without hesitation, she reciprocated.

"Was... anyone looking for me?"

Luca seemed as though confused by her question.

"Of course," he answered. "Your parents have organized search parties. It's been on the news every day. No one believed you just ran off."

She could feel her eyes welling with tears as she gazed out the window.

"I thought it was strange that Jim and Roxanne never helped in the searches," Luca continued. "I only kept working there to see if there was any trace of you. I knew *something* was off with those two, but this... I didn't see anything, not until the vanity."

"Yeah," June replied, trying in vain to mask her tears. "I thought they'd never let you back in the house."

"That was smart, June. You did good," he said, adjusting his grip on her hand.

"Thank you for coming," she said, managing a grin through the tears.

"Of course."

"How's your head?" she asked, realizing that nearly his entire shirt was now drenched in blood.

"It's been better... but I'll be fine. I never did see him coming."

"I know, me neither. I really thought you were dead... I wouldn't have been able to forgive myself."

"June, you have no idea how relieved I was to see your message written on the back of that vanity... just to know that you were *alive*. Just to know that you were *there*."

She smiled, though too embarrassed to respond.

CHAPTER EIGHTEEN

June took a moment to close her eyes as a medic carefully tended to her injuries. She and Luca had made it safely to the police station. She provided a brief statement before watching as at least a half-dozen officers rushed out of the station, headed to the home of Jim and Roxanne Wright. She had no idea what they might find once they'd made it there. *Did they get out in time? Did they escape through the backdoor? If they are alive, will they try to make it to the beach house? Would they come after me!?*

Luca was transported straight to the hospital upon their arrival, due to the blow he'd sustained to the head. June was assured by an officer that he was doing well under the circumstances.

The police station was quiet. She couldn't help but feel overwhelmed with emotion to have made it out of that house. Her feelings for Luca were now undeniable. He had risked his life to save hers, and they had made it out *together*.

She couldn't wait to get home, if only to sleep in her own bed again. She felt remorseful at the way she had behaved in the weeks leading up to her kidnapping. She had been selfish and arrogant. She had called her mother out for something which she knew nothing about. *I should have just asked her about the P.I. instead of unloading on her in front of Dad. She never had a chance to explain.*

"June?"

It was her mother. There she stood in the doorway. Her hair was wrapped loosely in a bun atop her head. She wore no makeup on her tear-stained face.

The medic who had been tending to June excused himself as Lorraine walked slowly into the room.

"Are you alright?" she asked, her voice shaking.

"Yes. I'm okay, Mom," she replied, standing to greet her.

Tears flowed freely as the pair embraced. June didn't know how to let go.

"Where's Dad?" she asked as they took a seat.

"He's on his way now. He was nearly an hour outside of town when we both got the call that you were here. We've been taking turns driving around looking for you... one of us always stayed home in case you showed up there."

"I see," June replied, still unable to contain her emotion.

"Who did this to you?" she asked, stroking her daughter's hair.

"The Wrights," she answered, feeling yet again ashamed for ever having trusted them.

Though clearly in shock, Lorraine remained silent as her daughter quickly detailed all that had transpired over the past month, yet stopped short of revealing *why* the Wrights had held her captive.

Lorraine held her head in her hands, unable to respond.

"I'm sorry, Mom. I'm so sorry."

"What could you have to be sorry for, June?"

"I'm sorry I trusted them. I'm sorry I didn't trust *you*," she answered solemnly. "I yelled at you right before I left... and I never gave you a chance. I'm sorry. This wouldn't have happened if it wasn't for me."

"It's not your fault. None of this is your doing. I shouldn't have been keeping a secret from you... or from your father," she responded, looking down at her lap. "The last time my father was in town he told me something... something that made me angry."

Lorraine took a deep breath before she continued, though never taking her eyes off the ground.

"He told me that he and my mom had adopted me as a baby... I never knew. I just felt betrayed, I guess... like my whole life has been a lie. You may have noticed him sending me those gifts lately, like the Fenton. He's been trying to apologize... but I didn't want to hear it."

June nodded, wondering how she'd ever muster the courage to tell her mother who Jim and Roxanne really were.

"I hired a P.I. to look for my birth parents...," Lorraine continued. "He hasn't been able to find them. I should have told you, and I'm sorry for that."

"No, it's okay, Mom."

"It's not... I've been distant toward you. I haven't been the mother I set out to be, not by a long shot. But when I saw your empty room that day, and you didn't come back... I realized I may never have the chance to make it up to you, and it nearly broke me."

"How did you know I didn't run away?" June asked.

"You may not realize it now, but your father and I know you better than that... it was *never* a question. The whole town has been looking for you non-stop – even Ethan Morris, if you can believe it."

"Ethan?" June repeated, cracking a smile.

"Yep, and all his friends, too. I guess they were the last ones to see you before you went missing. They came right away to tell us they'd seen you at Hank's that day. Ethan said you yelled at him, or something."

At this, the pair couldn't help but to laugh. She didn't know how long it had been since she'd been able to find humor in anything.

"Yeah, I guess he's not so bad," June quipped.

"We may have more help than we know what to do with at the shop pretty soon. I think your dad is going to let the boys work off their debt to society with some good old-fashioned manual labor, rather than pressing charges."

A female officer then entered the room. She had long, dark hair, and appeared to be in her mid-thirties.

"Hey guys, I just wanted to make sure you're doing okay in here. Do you need anything?" the officer asked warmly.

"I'm okay, thank you… but, have you heard anything about my friend? Luca?"

"The last I heard he's just being kept at the hospital overnight for observation. He should be just fine."

"And… the Wrights? Did they… I mean, do they have them?" she asked tentatively.

"I'm sorry. I'm just not sure on that. I *do* know that the fire department has been there a while trying to get everything under control. The whole house went up in flames," the officer responded **before taking her leave.**

"June, I don't want to press you too much on what all happened to you while you were in that house… what all happened *tonight*. I know you're exhausted. I just… I can't understand *why* the Wrights would take you. I can't understand why they would hurt you," her mother said, her voice quivering.

June then took her mother's hand gently into her own. "Mom… I have something I need to tell you about the Wrights."

Made in the USA
Monee, IL
11 May 2021